SIGHT

Nathan Sellers

Hugging Porcupines Press

AMERICAN FORK, UTAH

Doyle & Luann,
Thank you for coming and
joining the conversation. I hope this
book has helped in some way.

Nathan Sellers/Hugging Porcupines Press
P.O. Box 424
Midway, UT 84049
www.writingonpurpose.org

Publisher's Note: This is a work of fiction. Names, characters, places, and incidents are a product of the author's imagination. Locales and public names are sometimes used for atmospheric purposes. Any resemblance to actual people, living or dead, or to businesses, companies, events, institutions, or locales is completely coincidental.

Book Layout © 2017 BookDesignTemplates.com
Cover design by James Arrington – www.pukrufus.com
Author Photo – Mimi McDonald

Sight/ Nathan Sellers. -- 1st ed.
ISBN 979-8-9851998-1-9

To my wife, who fills me with feedback and encouragement.
And, to the Breakfast Club. You know why.

There's none so blind as they that won't see.

—JONATHAN SWIFT

The Afterlife

Summer 2021

Death approached through unfamiliar sounds in a perpetual blackness. Incessant, rhythmic beeps accompanied hushed voices to either side of Robert. Someone held his hand, gently stroking it. Drifting like a boat lightly tethered to the dock, Robert's consciousness betrayed him, drowning him in confusion.

"I wish I could see his face the moment he experiences color again," a male voice, deep and somber, spoke from the right.

Yes. A miserable life of blindness—robbed of what was most precious. *Just let me go now. Let this cursed blindness end.*

A vague memory of going to the hospital surfaced through the darkness of his mind. He was used to darkness—but this, somehow, was different. More disorienting.

"He lived a full life, despite everything."

"*He* wouldn't tell you that," responded a soothing, feminine voice. "He'd say it was half a life at best." There was sadness in that comment. Where did he know that voice? He strained at his memory, grasping at mist, finding nothing.

Beeping pressed into his awareness, pulling him back into the moment. The whispers ceased and the grip on his hand tightened. An alarm blared at the single, unbroken tone to the left as everything slipped away—everything except the grip on his hand. That remained, and somehow, felt more real.

"The transition here is going to be difficult."
"Yes," a soft voice whispered. "He's holding on to too much—and not enough."

Chapter 2

The Artwork

Spring 1984

Children laughed and splashed each other under the less-than-watchful eyes of parents casually eating their lunches by the fountains. The spring air pleasantly tickled the tall swaying palm trees like terre verte fan brushes painting a crystal blue sky. The excitement in the air was palpable--buzzing in anticipation of the fast-approaching Summer Olympics in Los Angeles. Everyone seemed to be talking about Russia's boycott, and what that would mean for America's athletes. New and beautiful buildings were finalizing their construction, and old ones were being renewed.

Robert, finishing his usual lunch outside the Los Angeles County Museum of Art, felt excitement bounce around his chest. Yet his excitement was not for the Olympics. Well, not really. He didn't care much for the politics and undercurrents of the Cold War. While it was fun to watch the competitions, that wasn't what he was looking forward to. The Olympics had created an opportunity for him.

The museum was opening a new exhibit as part of the Olympic Art Festival in June, only a few months away. He had worked hard as a member of the committee, striving to bring foreign, classical paintings to L.A. Because of those efforts, the committee had identified several French Impressionist paintings to feature. Now, the upcoming exhibit, "A Day in the Country:

Impressionism and the French Landscape," would be a fresh opportunity to stretch Robert's restoration skills on some recently discovered mid-nineteenth century pieces.

Cars drove past the LACMA along the Miracle Mile in splashes of cherry red, chrome yellow, brilliant orange, pastel white, and marina blue. But today, Robert watched for a familiar brown with gold lettering. He scheduled his lunch break during the typical noon delivery in hopes that he could be present when it arrived. Luck was drawing thin as he watched the tiny hands on his watch tick past the time he needed to return to work.

Oh well, he thought as he gathered up his Tupperware and walked back into the museum. Large shipments rarely occurred when expected; why would this one be any different?

Two hours later, after unproductive and unfocused work on various side projects, the page boy finally knocked on Robert's door, alerting him to the crate's arrival. In his excitement, he dismissed the young man and rushed through the museum like a schoolboy racing through the halls dodging the principal's watch. The crate stood alone in the receiving bay like a child waiting for a parent in an empty train station. Robert quickly strapped it onto a dolly and carted it up to his office.

The unboxing couldn't go fast enough. Anticipation gnawed at him, but he cautiously held back to avoid costly mistakes. This wasn't some birthday gift from childhood with an audience of eager eyes waiting to see what was behind brightly colored wrapping paper. There wasn't an audience at all. Just him, a wood crate, and a hammer and pry bar to get it open.

Robert paused. It was always more exciting to share this moment with someone. Briefly, the memory of his ex-wife standing with him for some of his first unboxings ran through his memory, flooding him with longing, loneliness, bitterness, and insecurity. Stuffing the unwanted feelings down, Robert walked to the phone and punched in his sister's number.

"Hello?" a soft, friendly voice answered.

"Sandra, it arrived."

"What arrived? Robert, is that you?"

"Yes. You know, the French piece that I've been telling you about. It arrived at the museum just a few minutes ago. I was about to open it up and wondered if you wanted to be here to see it." Robert tried to stifle his excitement.

"Oh, sorry Robert, I've got to pick up Bobby from school and take him to a soccer game in just a few minutes. There's no way I could come. Thanks for thinking of me though," Sandra said. Her voice was genuine, as always. "Let me know about it tonight. Are you coming over for dinner?"

"No. I'll probably work late," Robert answered, a little crestfallen. "I'm going to get the painting ready to start the restoration tomorrow. Thanks. Tell Bobby hi for me and give him a hug."

Sandra laughed. "Ok. Will do. Bye, Robert."

Robert hung up the phone in the cradle and looked around. He wanted to open it up, but the disappointment of not having anyone there to share the experience with slowed his movements. The loneliness pressed on him like a dark cloud, dampening the excitement.

He walked back to the table and began to work the pry bar to open the case. The top pulled away easily and revealed layers of styrofoam. The familiar smell of it reignited his enthusiasm.

A knock interrupted his work as he started to pull back the white, squeaky foam.

"Come in," Robert called out, now eager to see the painting.

A plain-looking woman with dark-rimmed glasses peeked through the door. Robert vaguely remembered her as one of the other restoration artists on the committee. He'd seen her in the halls before, but never really bothered talking to her.

"I heard the new painting arrived. Have you opened it yet?" she asked timidly.

Pushing away a twinge of initial annoyance at having been interrupted, Robert smiled politely. "Just opening it now." He wouldn't be alone for the reveal after all. That's what he wanted, right? Why had he been bothered when he had just interrupted himself to see if his sister could join him? Again, Robert pushed the thoughts and feelings aside and resumed pulling off the styrofoam.

"Come in. You can get the first glimpse of it with me."

The first thing he noticed was the smell of burnt wood and smoke. Surely it didn't *still* smell. It had been over fifty years since the fire. Excitement turned to worry as he gently removed the brown wrapping paper.

It was dark. The frame was charred all around the edges. Clearly, Robert would need to put in an order for a new frame. He worried about the extra time that would require. The dealer had explained this might be the case—the painting had been damaged in a fire, but that it was salvageable. Concern and irritation flooded him as he noticed a portion of the painting was almost completely obscured in smoke and grime. Was this even going to be worth the effort?

"Oh my!" the woman chirped, bringing her hand to her mouth. "You certainly have your work cut out for you. Would you like me to bring you some swabs?"

"No, thank you. I won't have time for cleaning today. I'll just remove the frame and get it prepped for tomorrow," Robert said.

"Ok," she said. She bent down and looked closely at the painting. "You can still see some of the color. I bet it's a beautiful painting." She smiled and looked up. The smile broke the plainness of her face. It somehow complemented her beige dress as her cheeks lifted her glasses.

"Yes. Beautiful," Robert said, momentarily distracted. He returned his gaze to the artwork. He hadn't seen any color. And yet, there it was. Some vague approximations of blue and green were peeking through. He could see outlines of trees, shadows contrasted against patches of light. How had he not seen the color? He was good at seeing color.

"Would you like any help before I go?"

"No, thank you. I can manage," Robert said.

"OK. Have a nice afternoon, Robert," the woman said, walking out of the office.

"You too," Robert replied, forgetting her name. He was embarrassed she had remembered his. He hoped she didn't notice the omission.

The frame was charred and disfigured. It had been intricately carved at one point in its life, but the detail crumbled at the touch. Black soot stained his fingers, a reminder to put gloves on before he handled the painting. Robert turned it over to look at the back. It wasn't a large painting, only about one and a half by two feet. The joints were in surprisingly good condition, and the back of the painting didn't show as many burn marks. Robert felt some relief as he realized that, while the painting was severely smoke-stained, it hadn't been burned. This was a good sign.

The rest of the afternoon was spent carefully removing the frame. He was surprised to see brighter colors around the edges of the canvas where the frame had protected it from the smoke. His usual excitement returned as truer colors were revealed. He mulled over whether he would need to remove the canvas. It wasn't as damaged as some of the other works he had restored in the past, though some punctures and a rip extended through the painting a few inches. Robert concluded the canvas would need to be removed from its stretching frame. He read over the commission agreement again for the restoration requirements.

"As much as possible without changing the integrity of the original painting," it read. He sniffed a bit at that. He wasn't an amateur. He would *never* compromise the integrity of the original painting.

Chapter 3

The Accident

January 1996

T hanks for showing us the new exhibit, Robert. It's really impressive," a young man in his mid-twenties said. A middle-aged woman, dressed in the fashion of the younger generation, stood by him smiling in agreement. All three stood several feet back from a large painting, admiring the artist's attention to light and color.

"Yes, thank you," the woman said. She stepped closer to Robert and whispered, "This is just what he needed. The breakup was really hard on him. He needed a good distraction."

"Well, it's my pleasure spending time with my favorite sister and nephew," Robert smiled at them.

"She's your only sister," Bobby said, smiling back.

"I admit, that *did* make it an easier choice." Robert looked back at the painting, squinting a bit. "I wish it was that easy to see the details on this piece."

"Put on your glasses then," Sandra chided.

"It's not the same. I miss the crispness I used to see. With glasses, there's always a glare on the inside of the lens. It's like looking through a window at a masterpiece but having it obscured by your own reflection."

"You guys are old," Bobby teased. "When I was your age—" he mocked in an old grandpa voice. Robert's teasing backhand to Bobby's stomach cut him off and he stepped back, laughing.

"Watch out you young whippersnapper, I've still got old man strength."

"Boys. They never grow up, even when they get older," Sandra muttered, rolling her eyes. "Seriously though, Robert, I hear you complain all the time about how you can't see stuff anymore. Isn't that kind of important for your work?"

"I see everything up close just fine. So it doesn't affect restoration work at all. It's only a problem when I step back to look at the whole piece," Robert answered.

"Sounds pretty important to me," Bobby chimed in.

"Well, have you tried contacts? That would fix the glare," Sandra asked.

"They don't make bifocal contacts," Robert grumbled. "My prescription doesn't work up close. Everything just goes fuzzy. It wouldn't work."

"Have you thought of LASIK?" Sandra said.

"Have I thought of whom?"

"Not a person. It's a new corrective eye surgery. It uses lasers, so it's more precise. It's just out of clinical trials. They say it can restore 20/20 vision. You should look into it."

"You want me to let a doctor shine lasers in my eyes…to *fix* my vision? That doesn't sound logical," Robert retorted. They walked along to the next painting, pausing again to appreciate the work. Squinting, Robert asked, "How much does it cost?"

"I'm not sure. Probably $2,500 or so per eye. Maybe a little more," Sandra said, no longer looking at the painting. She could tell his interest was piqued but wondered how he would react to the cost.

"Hmmph," he puffed, now looking back at Sandra. "Will insurance cover it?"

Sandra winced. "I'm not sure. I just heard about it recently. If I had to guess, I'd say probably not. It's still very new."

"What's the recovery time? If I did it, how long would I have to take off work?"

"That's the great thing about it, Robert. Because it's lasers, it's really precise. Most people are seeing clearly in a day or two. It's pretty remarkable." She was reeling him in.

"More than $5,000? Completely out of pocket? I don't have that kind of money just laying around. I think I'll stick to squinting."

Sandra's shoulders fell. She knew pressing the issue would probably have an opposite effect than she wanted. Instead, she walked close to him and put her arm around his waist. He looked down at her and instinctively wrapped his arm around her shoulder, giving her a hug. They held each other in silence, looking at the painting.

Robert broke the embrace, taking a few steps forward, arms behind his back, leaning in to the painting. "I love this one. The way the artist captures the sun's rays on the subject is just magical."

The trio walked around the gallery together for the rest of the afternoon. It was like a dance—side step, pause, step in, step back—waltzing through each room. They chatted and laughed, reflecting together in hushed, mostly reverent tones. As they exited into the main lobby, late afternoon sunlight shone through the windows.

"Robert," Bobby paused, looking at his uncle with a thoughtful intensity, "you're an art restorer."

"Last I checked."

"Funny. But seriously, your job requires your sight. You see things that my eyes just aren't trained to see. That's why I love coming to the art museum with you. You help me see things I wouldn't see otherwise. I appreciate the artwork so much more when I'm with you."

"Well, thank you," Robert said, a little surprised at Bobby's sudden sentimentality.

"But, I've been wondering, if I had come up to you earlier today and asked how much you would be willing to pay to have your sight completely restored, what would you have said? I mean, what's your sight actually worth to you?"

Chapter 4

The Afterlife

D arkness.

Darkness, but not…nothingness. There was still sensation, but different. He couldn't feel all the familiar aches and pains. Someone was holding his hand. Their hand was warm and squeezed him gently. He vaguely remembered someone holding his hand—in the hospital—right before he died.

"Am I still alive?" Robert whispered. As soon as he said it, he wondered why he had whispered. His voice felt strong, different. It didn't have the tightness he had grown used to. He took a breath and it came easily.

"No," a gentle but strong voice answered.

"Then why can't I see anything? I thought there was supposed to be some sort of light that I was supposed to go to. Everything is black."

"Sight is a curious thing," the voice returned. It was a woman's voice. Robert couldn't tell if he recognized it.

"Wait. So, I died, but I can't see? Am I in Hell? What did I do to deserve Hell?" Robert started to panic. Everyone had told him in the next life his sight would be restored. His blindness was *temporary* to *this* life.

"You are not in Hell, Robert."

"How can this not be Hell?" He raised his voice. "I lived twenty-five years of my life completely blind. That was my own personal Hell on earth. I looked forward to dying so many times because I would *see* again. And now, here I am, *dead*, and I still can't see? How is this not Hell?" Robert sat up, pulling his hand away from the woman. Trying to get his bearings, he realized he was in a bed. It embraced him with its softness. The ground did he same as he lowered his feet off the bed. Standing, Robert reached around, testing the air in from of him for any obstacles. He cautiously shuffled his feet making sure to not trip on anything. Was this carpet? It didn't feel like carpet, but it was gentle on his feet. It was like the ground *received* every step.

"How are you feeling?" the woman's voice asked.

"Awful," Robert retorted. "I can't see anything." He regretted the harshness of his voice as soon as he had said it. But it was true. How could he feel anything but awful after dying and *remaining* blind?

"I didn't ask how you were *seeing*. I asked how you were *feeling*," the woman responded, surprisingly calm.

"I'm sorry," Robert calmed himself. "I don't mean to be rude, but you've got to understand how shocking it is to still be blind. Or maybe you can't. You can probably see," he added, the bitterness creeping back into his voice.

"Yes, I can *see*," she emphasized the last word. "But Robert, I asked how you were feeling?"

"What do you mean? I answered you already. I'm *feeling* awful. Who are you anyway?" Robert asked, feeling annoyed at the repeated question.

"I am here to help guide you through the transition," the woman answered.

"Transition?"

"Yes. The transition from life to death. I could see it was going to be hard for you." Her voice was so calm, and almost cheerful. The familiarity of it itched at his consciousness, but he couldn't quite figure it out.

"Well, I'm glad you can see," Robert said sarcastically.

"Most people are surprised at how different the afterlife is from what they assumed. I'm here to help. Let's slow all this down. Pay attention to your sensations. A better question might be, *What* are you feeling? Close your eyes."

Robert scoffed. "What good will that do?"

"Just close them," she patiently insisted.

He closed his eyes. "Ok, now what?"

"Breathe."

"I'm dead. I don't need to breathe," Robert said sarcastically.

"A common misconception. Now Robert, slow down your mind and just breathe for a moment. See what you notice when you stop thinking and criticizing so much."

He did as instructed. Breathing felt normal, despite his deceased state. Or, maybe more accurately, it felt more like what normal *used* to be when he was younger and healthier. That was nice, but it didn't seem important. It's not like he would die if he stopped breathing. He wasn't going to enjoy the afterlife simply because he could breathe easily for eternity. Of all the senses to have restored—breathing?

"So, what am I supposed to be noticing?" Robert asked. She didn't respond. "Hello, are you still there? What am I supposed to notice?"

Silence.

This is ridiculous, Robert thought. *Twenty-five years of blindness. My world was taken away from me. Empty promises of a restoration. People just feeding my false hope so they didn't have to deal with my depression. And here I am, NOT enjoying the beauties and grandeur of heaven. The colors and shades and hues. It would have been better if there were no afterlife. Just oblivion. Nothingness. Not the continued torture of life without sight.*

"You still can't see it, can you?" the woman's voice returned. "Can't see anything through the fog and smoke of all your judgment, bitterness, and self-pity."

"No. I can't see anything. I'm blind. Still. I told you that," Robert lamented. "Are you here to rub my face in that? This has got to be Hell."

"Earthly concepts of Heaven and Hell are woefully inadequate. Forget what you think you knew about the afterlife. Time and immediacy are mortal concepts. Just be present."

"I think I'd rather not exist," Robert muttered darkly.

Warm hands grabbed the sides of his face. "Robert. Slow down. Breathe. Let go of your your self-pity. Break down your bitterness and wipe away your judgment. Just breathe and notice what *is*."

Robert was shocked at the intensity and kindness in her voice. Her hands remained on his face and for a moment, he realized how grounding it was. He took a breath. Robert had taken breaths before, even slow deliberate ones. But this one, with her hands on his face, was different. Focused. He didn't just feel her hands on his face, he experienced them.

"Your hands are warm, but not hot," Robert said.

"Good. Keep going."

"And your hands are soft and dry. Very comforting, and familiar. Do I know you?" Robert's mind strained at memories concealed behind a screen partition, taunting him.

"Stay focused, Robert."

He breathed again. Nothing. What was he supposed to be noticing? Was this some game in Hell? *Guess who?* Only no one needed to cover his eyes; they were permanently, and it seemed, eternally, closed.

"Look, this might be fun for you, but not for me. If you're here to taunt me, I've had enough. Just leave me alone," he said in despair. He heard a tired, sad sigh and the hands left his face. He immediately felt their absence. It was like something had been removed from his spirit, leaving a tangible void.

"It runs so deep," she whispered, her voice coming from somewhere in front of him. A quiet rumble sounded just beyond his ability to understand. "I can try, but it's like he doesn't even *want* to see."

Of course he wanted to see. What was she talking about? And who was she talking to?

"Robert, you are not in Hell. But you could make Heaven your own little Hell if you choose." Her voice was stern. "If you really want to stay blind, I will leave you to it. But it won't bring me, or you, any joy."

He wanted to retort, to complain about how joy had been taken away from him years ago, but he chose to remain quiet. His instincts to argue and defend pressed hard, begging to fight back while hiding behind walls to stop the pain of loss from sinking too deeply into his heart. He held them at bay, noticing emotions well up, threatening to spill over.

"What do you mean, stay blind?" he asked, throat tightening uncomfortably.

"I mean that here, in Heaven, your blindness is by choice."

"By choice?" Robert exclaimed, defenses returning. "You think I want to be blind? That I enjoyed it so much in life that I asked for the pleasure of darkness to remain through eternity? That is rich."

The sad sigh sounded again. No argument. No escalating voices.

"I know losing your sight was devastating. It ripped away the life and profession you knew," she began.

"Yes," he interrupted.

"But you need to learn to see in a way that you never really could if you want things to change," her voice trailed off.

Again, he shut off the angry quip that was his pattern in conversations like this. Why was he arguing? The pain of a sightless eternity was so raw that it squeezed at his heart, threatening to burst and bleed out years of suppressed emotion.

"Even when you could see, you were blind. And it's that sightlessness that keeps you blind now."

Chapter 5

The Artwork

Spring, 1984

It was so dark. As the canvas lay there, free from the stretching frame for the first time in years, Robert smiled. True, his initial impression had been shock, and even dismay at all the smoke damage, but he now stared down at the painting in excitement. These were the restoration projects that were the most exciting. The contrast between the before and after was stark if done right.

An eight-inch rip in the canvas, probably from something falling on it while in storage, had extended up into the frame. Removing the canvas had required extra caution to prevent further damage. Examining the edges of the tear, Robert worried that the force of whatever tore the canvas also stretched out the fibers. This would complicate a seamless repair.

The paint was cracked and loose around the tear leaving bare spots on the canvas. Precious details lost. This was not going to be an easy restoration.

The first step was always to clean the layers of filth from the surface of the painting. Cotton swabs and a neutralizer lay organized neatly to the side as he stretched his latex gloves tightly over his hands. He dipped a swab into the neutralizer and squeezed out the excess liquid.

Robert carefully tested a corner of the painting. Gentle swirls pulled away layers of dirt, grime, and smoke coating the painting. Robert examined the swab for any signs of varnish or paint. Satisfied that the neutralizer was safe, Robert continued cleaning the rest of the painting in slow circles.

A pile of darkened swabs lay to the side of the painting as Robert leaned in close to examine the revealed colors. While much of the painting was still dull and darkened, he was pleased with how much of the composition of light and shadow could now be seen. It was a classic composition, oriented horizontally, with the lower-left portion in dark, blue-green shadow, following a path up into the light shining down through the trees in the upper right of the painting.

A placard on the back of the painting confirmed the details that Robert had been given by the owner. It read:

Le Chemin du Jardin
Adenet DuPois, 1867

The brush strokes were thick and layered in some areas providing a rich texture, characteristic of the beginning of the French impressionist era. While the texture enhanced the style of the painting, it would prove to be more challenging in the restoration process. Robert was accustomed to the typical smooth texture of older oil paintings that didn't require the same level of artistry when restoring areas of paint loss. He was both apprehensive and excited about the prospect of working on this project. It would definitely be a learning endeavor to bolster his resumé of skills.

With the surface cleaned, Robert could see that the varnish had significantly yellowed the painting and absorbed much of the smoke coating the surface. Though the process to remove the varnish was slow and tedious, it was also quite rewarding to discover the true colors the artist had used, and see it the way the artist intended for the first time in over a century.

Even though Robert knew that the removal of the old varnish would give the clearest picture of true colors, he was always surprised at how much just a simple washing did to reveal the painting beneath.

Chapter 6

The Accident

October 1996

The doorbell rang. His heartbeat immediately raced as he paced back and forth in his room. Silly. He shouldn't be nervous. The doctors had reassured him that the procedure was safe and the recovery period short. But here it was; today was the day. He was really going through with it. Would years of fruitless squinting really be gone? He had his doubts, but that didn't stop him from the flashes of hope and excitement of being able to see clearly again.

Robert double-checked he had everything he needed. He patted down all of his pockets, looking around the kitchen for anything he may have forgotten. The doorbell rang again. He rushed to the door.

"There you are." Sandra's smiling face greeted him. "I was starting to think you might have chickened out."

"Funny," Robert said flatly. "I was just checking to make sure I didn't forget anything."

"What could you possibly forget? This is a same-day procedure. It's not like you needed to pack anything," Sandra teased. "Come on, everything is going to be fine. Stop worrying so much."

They walked out to the car, still running in the driveway. It was a tan Honda Civic, the most generic car Robert could imagine. It didn't match his sister's personality at all. She was always smiling and full of life. She wore bright colors and tried to stay up to date with the current fashions. Sandra had always been this way; it was no wonder she had been popular in school. Not because she was pretty—which she was, though Robert never bothered letting her know—but because she was so warm and welcoming to everyone.

"Still driving this old thing?" Robert said as he sat down in the passenger seat.

"Absolutely. It's not pretty to look at, but it's just so practical, I can't let it go."

They slowly backed down the driveway, Sandra twisting awkwardly as she looked out the back window. She slammed the breaks just as she got to the curb, jerking Robert forward and locking his seatbelt around his chest.

"Did you remember your insurance card?" Sandra asked, looking intently at him.

"Jeez, woman! You about gave me a heart attack," Robert breathed out. "Of course I remembered my card. They reminded me at least three times at the initial visit."

"Well, I just wanted to make sure. It'd be a shame to get there and have to delay the surgery just because you didn't remember your insurance card."

Robert closed his eyes and shook his head. She had ended up so much like their mother. A worrier about the simple stuff, but calm as can be when things got serious. He felt a pang of loss at the memory of his mother.

"What?" Sandra asked defensively.

"Nothing," Robert replied, with a little defensiveness in his tone as well. "You just reminded me of Mom."

"Well, thank you. She was a truly wonderful woman," Sandra replied, sitting up a little taller in her seat. She continued backing up the car into the street.

"Yes, she was."

The waiting room at the LASIK Center was stale. The beaded chain tying the pen to the clipboard clacked obnoxiously as Robert struggled to fill out the required paperwork.

"They never make these things long enough," Robert complained.

"What?" Sandra asked absentmindedly as she read a TIME magazine flashing a front cover with the smiling faces of Diane Keaton, Bette Midler, and Goldie Hawn.

"The stupid chains. You can hardly write when you get to the bottom of the page."

"Hmm," Sandra mumbled, obviously reading some fascinating article.

"Wait, what? You've got to be kidding me," Robert muttered. "Potential risks: Dry eye syndrome, Debilitating visual symptoms, Loss of vision. And they want me to sign a legal waiver?"

Sandra, alert now, put her magazine down and looked at the legal forms. "They just have to include everything that could happen. You know that. I'm sure you have legal forms you give clients when you restore their artwork so they can't sue you, right?"

"Yeah, but I'm not telling them they could go blind if they have me restore their artwork."

Sandra stifled a laugh. "That's not fair, Robert. The doctor is working with your eyes, not a piece of canvas."

"I know, but I'm here to *improve* my vision, not lose it."

"It'll be fine. Loads of people are having this done with remarkable results," Sandra said. "Just sign the papers and give it back to the lady already."

Robert rolled his eyes and finished filling out the paperwork and returned it to the receptionist. She glanced through it.

"Thank you. We'll call you up when the doctor is ready for you," she said routinely. "You did bring someone to drive you home, right?"

"Yes, my sister is here," Robert said, indicating towards Sandra, still reading the magazine.

"Mm kay," she replied smiling. "You won't be able to drive home, and probably shouldn't even try driving tomorrow."

"Of course," Robert said stiffly as he returned to his seat. His heart raced and his legs tingled. He hated waiting. It was even worse as he considered the risk he was taking. This was his eyes. Lasers burning his eyes. It was like a sculptor having surgery on his hands. What if something went wrong? His eyes were his livelihood.

"Relax," Sandra said, placing her hand on his bouncing knee. "It's going to be fine."

"Easy for you to say. It's not *your* eyes."

"Just breathe, Robert. The success rate is really high," Sandra reassured. "Remember, you're the one who agreed to this. You did your research. It's going to be fine."

"I know," Robert consented. "But that doesn't help right now."

"Well," Sandra probed, "do you want to talk about it?"

"No," he sighed. "That just makes it worse."

They sat together in silence, interrupted only by the occasional turn of a page, the receptionist tapping away at her computer, and Robert's bouncing leg. After about ten minutes that felt more like an hour, a nurse stepped into the waiting area and called Robert back. Sandra gave him a reassuring tap on his leg and a thumbs up for good measure.

"Alright," the doctor said from behind his mask, "that's it."

"It's done?" Robert asked.

"Yep," he said, his smile showing through his eyes. "Not too bad, is it?"

Robert marveled at the quickness of the procedure as the doctor and nurses removed the equipment from his eyes. The lasers had only been at each eye for just a short time, maybe only minutes. It hadn't been painless like some had told him, but it hadn't been terrible either. He sat up and looked around.

"Everything is so clear!" Robert said, surprised. "Does it really work that quickly?"

"Well, yes and no," a nurse replied. "Most patients have very clear vision immediately following the procedure, but that only lasts a short while. The healing process will take a day or two. Your eyes will get blurry while the tissues repair. That's why we make sure you have someone to take you home."

"If it ends up being like what it is now, this is a miracle," Robert said as he looked across the room, easily reading signs and posters.

"You'll want to take it easy for a couple days," the doctor noted. "Your eyes are going to be fairly uncomfortable. They'll be dry and scratchy. Don't scratch them, obviously. We'll give you plenty of drops to help keep them wet." He liberal applied solutions to Robert's eyes. "Do you have any questions?"

"So, was it a success? Did everything go right?"

"Yes sir," the doctor smiled at him. "It was a textbook operation."

"Anything I should watch out for?"

"First and foremost, just take it easy for the next couple of days. Stay in darker rooms and wear sunglasses if you have to be outside. Do your best to not rub your eyes. We'll give you some plastic shades for your drive home." The nurse left the room for a moment and returned with a curled strip of black plastic with a notch for a nose. She handed them to him. "Try these on."

Despite being cheap, they worked surprisingly well. The nurse gave him a packet of papers with explanations of symptoms to watch out for and reminders of the proper care for his recovery. She escorted him from the operatory back to the waiting room. In that short span, Robert could notice the clarity he initially felt was starting to fade into fuzziness.

"Hey, Stevie Wonder," Sandra said, setting down her magazine. "How did it go?"

"Surprisingly well. The doctor said it was textbook," Robert said.

"Can you tell a difference? I mean, can you see through walls now or anything?"

Robert chuckled. "I think that would be a bit too much. Remember, it's the walls that I was trying to see in the first place."

"Seriously though, how's your sight?" Sandra probed again.

"Well, right when it was done, it was really great. I could read everything on the walls. But that's starting to fade now," Robert explained. "But they said that was normal; that it would take a couple days to let my eyes recover."

"But it will go back to being clear though, right?" Sandra asked.

"That's what they said."

"That's so great, Robert," Sandra said, hugging him. "See, I told you everything would be fine."

"And there it is," Robert smiled sardonically. "I was just waiting for the 'told you so'."

"Well, I mean, when you're right you're right. Am I right?"

They checked out with the receptionist, setting a follow-up appointment for a few days away. Robert's eyes continued to get scratchier as they walked to Sandra's car. They felt as if someone had thrown sand in them; Robert fought the temptation to rub them. He pulled out the drops as he sat down in the passenger seat, hoping for some relief. Awkwardly, he dripped them into each eye, but that only seemed to make them burn a bit more.

"I'm glad you're the one driving," Robert said. "I'm sure we'd never make it there if it were me."

Chapter 7

The Afterlife

Soft grass caressed his feet. At least, he thought it was grass. Whatever it was, it was soft. His companion was leading him somewhere, holding him gently by the crook of his elbow. She had stopped talking to him again and he was content with the fact. It's not like their conversations had been productive, or even pleasant. Every time she mentioned anything about his sight, his jaw instinctively clenched and his heart pumped with defensive adrenaline. She was so insensitive, accusing him thoughtlessly and failing to understand how difficult his life had been.

A cool breeze tickled across his skin. Sunshine radiated a warmth, reminding him for a moment of his childhood. His family used to go on walks in his childhood, parents walking hand in hand as he and his sister ran off the trail, chasing one another through the tall grass of a meadow. He loved those days. Everything always seemed so happy and right. Even that didn't last.

After walking sightlessly for what seemed like ages, his guide stopped him in the shade of something large. He felt pressure pulling down gently on his elbow and he guessed she wanted him to sit. He obliged. Doing so was much easier than before, joints responding smoothly without any pain. At least something was working correctly.

"Robert," the woman's gentle voice began again, "your life was filled with good things."

His eyebrows raised questioningly. "My life? Filled with good things? You obviously haven't been peering down from the clouds very closely. Or maybe you're blind too and I've just come to the place where blind people go after they die."

"No Robert, I can see quite clearly, and I have paid very close attention to your whole life. And I can say, quite assuredly, that your life was filled with good things."

"Well, I guess you stopped paying attention the last twenty-five years," Robert said. He didn't want to argue with her, but she was just so wrong.

"If you insist on staying stuck in your blindness," she said. "we'll need to appeal to your other senses for a while. Humor me for a moment, Robert, and stop trying to see everything through those blind eyes of yours."

"I stopped doing that years ago," Robert muttered.

"Yes, you did. Even before your eyes went dark, you struggled to see clearly," she countered. "And I'm not talking about your myopia."

"Then what *are* you talking about?" Robert's tone was hard, though he was genuinely curious. This wasn't the first time someone had told him he *wasn't seeing* things. Painful memories of past relationships attempted to bubble up through his consciousness. Reflexively, he pushed them away and turned his head in the direction he guessed the woman was sitting. Softer now, he asked, "What am I not seeing?"

"Our sight has so much to do with what we choose to pay attention to. You know this. Your profession depended on your focus on detail. You *saw* things that others didn't simply because you trained yourself to pay attention to those specific details. You studied in school to understand more clearly the things your eyes were seeing in an artwork."

Robert's mind easily drifted to his time at The School of Art Institute of Chicago. He could hear his professors in his early classes of figure drawing and basic drawing exclaim, "Draw what you see, and not what you know, until that happy day that you know what you are seeing." He remembered how transformative that statement had been for him, allowing him to pay more attention to what he was actually seeing. He had been shocked at everything he had to unlearn from his youth spent drawing people and faces. Despite being acknowledged as a great artist in high school, art school truly opened his eyes to what was really in front of him. Over and over again, professors shattered his artistic paradigms, creating new horizons.

"OK," Robert consented, "I'm listening."

"I was surprised at how you never really learned to use your other senses to see. Most people, when they go blind, learn to rely on them. Their senses become more heightened and sometimes they see things better than when they had their vision."

"You keep saying they can see better," Robert interrupted. "Clearly, if they're blind, they can't see better."

"Not visually, no," she replied. "And that's where you keep getting stuck, Robert. There's so much more to sight than vision."

Robert leaned back, extending his arms to prop him up. Grass stuck up through his fingers, cool and slightly damp. He could feel the small blades poking softly at his palms. He had always enjoyed sitting in the grass under the shade of some tree, watching clouds pass or branches sway in the wind. He missed those simple pleasures so deeply that he felt himself hardening in the sadness of the loss.

"A mother doesn't need to see her child crying to know he's unhappy," The woman continued, watching Robert wrestle with what she was saying. "The cry itself is enough. And with even more attention to the cry, a mother can know if the child is hungry, tired, sad, or hurt. This attention is important to a mother's sight, or understanding, even without seeing the child with her eyes. The different tones and volumes invite her to act in different ways. Many a new mom has been frustrated in her attempts to soothe her baby, seeing the distress with her eyes, but failing to understand the cause with her ears.

"So, lay back for a moment. Pick one of your senses and just notice all you can. Let it paint the image in your mind."

Reluctantly, Robert lowered himself to lay on his back. He extended his arms to the side, stretching his muscles. They felt strong and loose. How long had it been since he had felt such ease of movement?

He decided to focus on his sense of touch. "OK, I can feel the grass."

"What about the grass?" the woman prodded. "How does it feel?"

"It's cool, like it would feel in the early morning, shortly after the sun rises. Damp, but not wet." He brushed his fingers slowly through the blades, stopping occasionally and rubbing individual blades through his fingers. He noticed when he stroked the blade towards the earth, it had a rough, almost sticky texture. However, sliding back up towards the tip, it was smooth. Was this a different kind of grass, or had he just never noticed that texture?

A gentle breeze swept over the grass, causing it to move ever so slightly, bumping against his arms and hands. He imagined it like a brief, impromptu dance of petite, emerald dancers, finishing almost as soon as they started.

Pressing down harder, the earth beneath the grass was lumpy. Not hard and stiff like a vole infested lawn, but soft, like a freshly tilled and planted garden. He poked at it with his fingers, enjoying how it yielded to his touch. The soil stuck to his skin as he pressed it between his thumb and forefinger. It was slightly grainy, and clumps fell as he circled his fingers rhythmically.

"Hmm. What are you noticing, Robert?"

"The dirt," he replied.

She chuckled, "Yes, I can see that. And only a moment ago you waxed so poetic. Where did the detail, the *attention* go?"

"I'm noticing the texture of the soil and the grass." Robert paused. "I didn't realize there was so much I'd never paid attention to," he said.

"I wouldn't say never, but it has been a very long time," the woman returned. "You used to be more curious."

Robert wondered how she knew such a detail from his life. She was right, though. As a child, he had always been full of questions and imagination. He would run, explore and laugh.

The innocence of youth had blessed him with simple joy. Even in high school, as the Civil Rights movements began to escalate through the country and tensions grew, Robert maintained his attention and wonder to the world around him. Art had been his escape, his expression, and passion. Colors and shapes, shades, and hues were exciting. He had friends whose parents purchased new color TVs. While they would gather around in awe at the new technology, the color on the television set was never quite as rich as what life had to offer. Being outside—taking in the greens and blues, lights and shadows—this was what Robert loved.

This passion for color and imagination followed him into college, igniting further exploration and interest. Yet, he was also on his own for the first time, faced with the reality of adult life. Conversations regarding the Cold War, the space race, international tensions, and local debates on segregation and racism tugged and jockeyed for his attention. He wanted to be a responsible citizen, informed and moral. But the attitudes of fear, competitiveness, and hate robbed him of innocence. He needed to be *mature*. And so, Robert's natural curiosity slowly melted into a pool of seriousness. Only art could recapture that light in his eyes.

"Robert, you are an artist, so I know there was more to your experience with touch than just the physical sensations on your skin," the woman eased in gently, testing Robert's openness to seeing another perspective, to admitting that his blindness had not robbed him of everything. "You lived a life full of visual imagery. You immersed yourself in the richness of it all. That can't have gone away."

"My life wasn't *full* of visual imagery. It was cut short," Robert said, though softly, almost to himself.

"Yes, Robert, your vision was cut short, but your memory of it was not," she returned, matching his soft tone. "But the devastation and bitterness you felt, and continue to feel, about your loss have darkened that memory, almost as much as your eyes were darkened to any light."

She reached out and gripped his hand in hers. Stroking the back of his hand, she continued, "That memory of light and color isn't gone. It just needs your attention once again. It needs you to wipe away the betrayal of sadness and bitterness. There is more to sight than seeing, Robert."

With a sigh, Robert slumped his shoulders and nodded. Again, she was right. He was tired of arguing with her. His mind *had* been filled with the memory of color and light. But the memory hurt. It was a constant reminder that he couldn't see anymore—couldn't create new memories—have new experiences. Those were the lies he told himself to push away the pain.

"We all have pain in life, Robert," she continued. "But we have to choose what we focus on. Will we feed our pain by focusing on how much it hurts? Or, can we embrace it and then heal by focusing on what we still have? The cure for bitterness is gratitude. It's like a soap that can scrub away the grime of resentment. And you have much to be grateful for."

"Like what?" Robert questioned, a hint of bitterness returning to his voice.

"Oh, I can't give it all to you," she explained. "Gratitude isn't found by others telling you the good in your life. It only comes from your noticing it, tasting it, and acknowledging the blessings that produce it."

Robert ran his fingers through his hair. It was full, thick hair. Quite different from the thin strands he had spent the last few decades fretting over. *Well, that's nice,* he thought. At least hair was restored in the afterlife.

"Think hard, Robert. What was the good in your life?"

He laid back again and reflected on his life. Wave after wave of frustrations, disappointments, and pain crashed on his mind. Filtering through the negative was like trying to build a sandcastle near the shore break. Every handful of positive memories was quickly washed away in some complaint or associated negative event. Hopelessness grew as he struggled with what seemed like a losing battle. Years of allowing the negative to permeate each thought had shaped him into a curmudgeon. Why had he not noticed this in himself? Why had the negatives been so important to him?

His mind rested on his time working at the art museum. He loved that job. Every day was an adventure in bringing to light a past that had been lost or clouded. There were challenges in the work, sure, but that had been more like a puzzle to be solved instead of a barrier. To bring something back to its original state for the enjoyment of the viewer was a joy, often made richer because of the work he had done to get it there.

"I loved my job," Robert admitted, this time pushing down the resentment at having lost it due to his blindness. "It was one of the great blessings in my life."

"Hmm, yes it was," the woman said, warmly. "How did you get that job?"

The question surprised him. He hadn't thought much about what led him to the museum. He moved to Los Angeles in the early months of 1970 at his sister's suggestion. Weighed down by the searching eye of the Vietnam draft and the coldness of a bitter divorce, the streets of New York had felt oppressive to him. He imagined every eye on him, judging and condemning him. Sandra had noticed the change in his voice as they talked over the phone and worried, as she usually did, about him. She had stayed in Southern California to be near their mother. He always thought this was because she was a homebody and couldn't leave, but now, he realized she stayed to care for their mother.

Los Angeles turned out to be exactly what he needed. The warm weather and sunshine in the winter seemed to thaw the coldness that was settling on his heart. The job hunt was slow, but he hadn't felt the financial pressure since Sandra allowed him to live with her and her new husband. It was awkward at first, as he felt like an intruder into their marriage, but he quickly learned that Tom, her husband, was just as open and welcoming.

Robert's resume was one of the best due to his Master's degree from New York University, The Conservation Center of the Institute of Fine Arts. He had made many sacrifices to get into the school, and had needed help financially. The sacrifices of his mother hit him deeply. He remembered the exhausted look on her face that she couldn't hide each summer he was home. He felt the guilt afresh as she gave him cash to help pay tuition. Yet through those emotions, somehow he had managed to take her sacrifice for granted. He winced at the entitled attitude of his younger self. He winced again with the realization that he had never really changed his perspective while she was alive.

Robert was embarrassed. Embarrassed that he focused so intensely on *his* needs and emotions that he failed to see his mother's until it was too late. His mother had been an angel—so positive and resilient. She gave her everything to each of her children, and all he managed to notice was what was going wrong.

He wanted to scream at himself for what he had lost—not his sight nor his mother—the opportunity to recognize and thank her for all she had done for him. He vowed to himself that if he ever got the chance to interact with her here in the afterlife that he would meet her with the gratitude he should have shown her while she was alive.

"I get what you're saying," Robert said softly. "I looked over the positives, not seeing the blessings in it. My mother was so good to me, always giving so I could have a better life. And I didn't recognize it like I should have."

The woman grabbed his hand again, squeezing it between both of hers. She didn't say anything, but he could feel a warmness and love coming from her.

"The hard part is," Robert continued, "there was just such a constant barrage of bad. I couldn't enjoy the good because so many challenges overshadowed it."

He expected the woman to argue with him. To tell him he had chosen to pay more attention to those things. But she didn't. She just held his hand tighter.

"You did have an uncommon amount of hardships, didn't you?" she said compassionately.

"Yes," Robert answered, choking the sudden emotion back, shocked at her empathy, "I did."

"Will you tell me about it?"

"Shouldn't I be focused on "all the good" in my life?" he asked, making quotes in the air with his fingers.

"We'll get to that," the woman answered. "For now, why don't you tell me about how hard things were."

And so he began. These memories came much easier.

Chapter 8

The Accident

October 1996

The sun glared brightly as they pulled out of the parking garage, its rays stabbing at Robert's tender eyes. He closed them reflexively and leaned back against his headrest. He put his usual sunglasses on over the top of the flimsy shades the LASIK center had given to block the light even further. Despite the pain, Robert was relieved the procedure had gone well. The short glimpse of seeing the walls so clearly had been encouraging. He thought about walking through the museum and being able to see the details in each painting, the tightness of the colors, and how they worked in harmony with one another. He allowed himself to be excited.

"Sandra," Robert started.

"Hmm?" Sandra replied absentmindedly, looking both ways before pulling out onto the street.

"Thank you."

"For what?" she asked, settling into her lane, matching the speed of the other motorists.

"For all of this," he said. "For suggesting to have this procedure done. For driving me here and waiting, and now driving again. I really appreciate it."

"Oh," Sandra said, surprised at his uncharacteristic gratitude and positivity. She placed her right hand on his knee. "Well, of course I would do all that. That's what siblings do for each other, right? I mean, you would have done the same for me."

"Right," Robert answered, wondering if he actually would have. "But I still appreciate it."

"Well, you're welcome. I'm happy to do it."

Her cheery disposition was always a comfort to him, especially in the times he didn't feel it himself. It had always been that way, even when they were little kids. She was outgoing and positive, a believer in people. She could make friends with anyone, and each person always seemed to feel like they were important to her. And the truth was, they were. She genuinely valued people, warts and all. He, on the other hand, was an introvert. It was hard for him to smile and engage so openly. He was always evaluating what was going on around him and trying to make sense of it and figure out how to respond. It wasn't that he didn't value people, he just preferred to do so one at a time.

Sandra pulled onto the I-5 southbound, merging slowly into the congested L.A. traffic. Robert closed his eyes, allowing Sandra to navigate the road.

"Would you like to listen to some music? It's probably going to be another twenty minutes before we get to your house," Sandra asked.

"Sure, whatever," Robert answered, adding, "As long as it's not country. I value my ears too much."

Sandra smacked his leg. "It's not that bad, Robert."

He smiled as she turned on the radio and adjusted the dial. Scanning through the stations they caught snippets of several songs: *Return of the Mack* (change the station, please), *The Beautiful People* by Marilyn Manson (creepy), *Wannabe* by the Spice Girls (change it quick before it gets stuck in my head), before finally settling with Eric Clapton's new song, *Change the World*. His soulful voice was a welcome accompaniment to the drive.

They remained on the freeway for the duration of the song and two others, silently enjoying the music together. Robert kept his eyes closed and his head back, trying to manage the discomfort. Eventually, Sandra exited the freeway, eager to be out of the stop-and-go traffic.

"How have things been going for you lately, Robert?" Sandra asked, trying to spark up some conversation.

"Fine," he replied.

"Ugh," she breathed out in exasperation, "Do I always have to spell it out?"

"Spell what out?" Robert asked. "I said things have been fine."

"Are you seeing anyone?"

"Not right now, my eyes are closed," Robert joked, straight-faced.

Sandra shook her head, clearly not amused. "Seriously, Robert. Have you been going on dates? Are there any women out there that you're interested in?"

Robert took a long, slow breath through his nostrils before responding. "You worry about me too much, Sandra. I'm a bit too old to enter that game now. I'm perfectly content—"

The car lurched forward as Sandra slammed on the brakes. Robert's eyes snapped open just quick enough to see a ruby sedan smash into their front end. Everything was chaos. His head slammed into the dashboard, and he could feel blood trickling down his face where his glasses had cut into his skin. He wasn't sure if the car was spinning or if it was just his head. All he could hear was a dull ringing. His legs were pinched under the dashboard, though thankfully, he could still move them.

He turned to check on Sandra, but the bright light of the day was too much for his eyes without the dark glasses that had fallen off when he hit his head. He groaned and laid his head back against the headrest.

"Robert, are you OK?" Sandra's voice was weak but worried.

"I'm fine," he replied instinctively. "What about you?"

"My neck really hurts, and the steering wheel is digging into my legs."

Worry rose in his stomach. The cheeriness and optimism were gone from her voice. She was in real pain. He didn't dare venture to open his eyes again; instead, he reached out to his left, feeling for her. Finding her arm, he squeezed it.

"It's going to be OK. I'm right here," he said, trying to stay calm. His hand traveled down her arm and found her hand. It was wet. She winced and pulled away.

"I've got glass in my knuckles," she explained. "I think they hit the windshield."

Voices approached outside the car from multiple directions. They knocked at the side windows, asking if they were OK. Robert knew they weren't, but without opening his eyes, he couldn't tell how bad. Through the pain of the light, he cracked his eyes open. The hood of the car obscured the view through the shattered windshield. What looked like smoke or perhaps steam spilled out from the front of the car. Worried faces peered through the windows, working to open the doors. It was all too much. The light, the feel of sandpaper in his eyes, the throbbing of his head and neck; Robert closed his eyes to the nightmare.

Sirens of emergency vehicles sounded in Robert's ears before paramedics arrived with a barrage of questions. They carefully fitted him with a C-collar before pulling him out of the wreckage. Robert and Sandra were placed in separate ambulances, leaving behind the carnage of the two smashed cars.

"How is my sister?" Robert asked the paramedic attending to him. He could tell they were driving fast, though there was no siren.

"She is being taken care of, don't worry. How are you feeling?" the paramedic replied, trying to fall back into his routine of questions.

"No, that doesn't answer my question. Is she OK? She was bleeding and had glass in her hands," Robert said, feeling worry boil up to the surface.

"You're bleeding too," the paramedic replied, dodging the question. "Do you know what cut your eyebrow?"

"Probably the dashboard," Robert replied, frustrated at his question being deflected.

"Were you wearing glasses at all?" he probed. "You also have a cut on your nose that's consistent with someone wearing glasses."

Robert remembered the shades he had placed over the dark plastic the LASIK Center had given him. "Yes, but they were just sun shades. I just had LASIK surgery this morning and I was trying to protect my eyes from the light."

"Well, it looks like they may have protected you from more. Be grateful you didn't get any glass in your eyes," the paramedic replied. "Do you mind if I check your eyes? I'll turn down the lights first."

Robert consented, opening his eyes slowly after the cabin lights were out. It was painful, but not as bad as the direct sunlight had been. Equipment beeped and flashed all around him, crimson and cerulean. Cords swayed with the rocking of the vehicle as it bounced along towards the hospital.

"Sorry, but I'm going to need to shine the light in your eyes to check for a concussion," he stated, bringing up a small flashlight just over his right eye.

The light seared, and Robert reflexively squinted. The paramedic switched between eyes, apologizing each time Robert winced.

"Well, the good news is that you don't seem to have a concussion. Your eyes are pretty red and bloodshot, though I imagine that's from the surgery."

"And the bad news?"

"You're probably going to have a matching pair of shiners to show off for a couple of weeks," the young paramedic said as he started to slip a blood pressure cuff around Robert's arm.

"Can you please tell me how my sister is doing?" Robert pleaded again.

"I'm sorry, sir. I don't know. I was attending to you at the scene and didn't take a close look at her," he apologized. "But I can tell you she's in good hands."

Robert relented his questioning. The rest of the ride was spent in silence except for the occasional sound of the siren as they approached each intersection. Before long, the ambulance stopped and the back doors opened. Robert closed his eyes tighter against the light as they wheeled him into the hospital.

In the ER, Robert submitted to doctors poking and prodding and shining lights painfully into his eyes. X-rays were taken of his neck. A thoughtful nurse brought him a pair of shades to replace the ones that had been lost in the accident. Everything seemed like a whirlwind; he grew tired and achy now that the shock and adrenaline from the crash had worn off.

"Here you are," a strong male voice spoke through the doorway. "You were much harder to find than Sandra, though I'll admit I looked a bit harder for her."

A tall, olive-skinned man with sun-bleached blond hair came in and sat next to Robert. Cautiously, he ventured a peek at the man. He looked like the classic California surfer type, though his hair was short and well-groomed.

"Hey, Tom," Robert said, relieved to see Sandra's husband. "How is Sandra?"

"Oh, I think she's fine," he said. "She probably looks worse than she is due to the glass cutting up her hands, but the doctors say that should heal up in a couple of weeks. She's worried sick about you though. She's been asking the doctors about you and sent me to track you down."

"I was sure she had broken bones or internal bleeding or something. They had to break the steering wheel to get her out of the car."

"Well, she does have quite a bit of bruising," Tom explained. "But the x-rays all came back clear. She's really fortunate."

"I don't know if I would use the word *fortunate* to describe what we've been through," Robert said, wincing a little as he sat up in his bed.

"Sandra feels terrible, as you can imagine. She keeps beating herself up over the accident and is worried about your eyes." Tom looked intently at Robert. "How are they? Your eyes, I mean?"

"They feel about the same as they did after the surgery," Robert said. "They're super sensitive to light, hence the super-stylish shades. It feels like someone threw sand in them, but the

LASIK people said that would happen. Mostly I've just been keeping them closed because it hurts a whole lot less than when they're open."

"Did the doctors check them out at all? I mean, you did just have surgery on them."

"The paramedics looked at them more often than was comfortable," Robert grimaced. "They didn't say anything other than that I didn't seem to have a concussion. They did say I was lucky that I had the glasses on as that probably protected me from getting any glass in my eyes."

"Well, that's lucky, I guess. Sandra said you had blood running down your face," Tom said. "She thought maybe your eye had been cut open. She's worried she messed everything up."

Robert pulled down his glasses to show Tom the gash across his eyebrow and nose. "You can let her know that the only thing she messed up is my perfect good looks. Probably won't be going on a lot of dates with a face like this."

Tom laughed. "She'll be relieved. Now she'll have an undisputed claim as the most attractive person in your family."

Robert laughed too, but quickly stopped because it hurt too much. "Well, don't tell her I said this, but she's been the clear winner of that title since the day she was born."

"I heard that," Sandra said, limping into the room.

"Hey," Tom exclaimed, rising to his feet. "I told you to not go anywhere without me."

"Well, I told the doctors I was fine and that I really needed to see my brother, who is clearly less attractive than me," she said as Tom helped her into the chair he had been sitting in. "They couldn't have kept me down if they tried. Robert, how are your eyes?"

"Better than your hands," Robert said, looking at the gauze wrappings that made them look like an Egyptian mummy.

"Oh, these will be fine," Sandra said, holding them in the air. "But really, Robert, I feel terrible. What did the doctors say?"

"They shone a lot of lights in them which was clearly uncomfortable. They didn't seem to care that my eyes were hypersensitive from the LASIK procedure. They did notice the laser incisions, but only barely commented on it. They just confirmed what the paramedics had told me in the ambulance; I don't seem to have a concussion."

Robert paused for a moment looking down at Sandra's hands and then the worried and guilty look on her face. "It'll probably be fine. It could have been much worse. I'm just thankful that my hands don't look like yours. I can't imagine how hard it would be to do my job if they were all sliced up like yours. I mean," he held up his hands, "these are my tools."

Chapter 9

The Afterlife

I wish I hadn't been born on Thanksgiving."

"Why?" the woman asked, surprise in her voice.

"It's just that bad things always seemed to happen around my birthday and Thanksgiving Day. I stopped looking forward to both," Robert explained. "People would remind me to be grateful, but they always seemed to tell me that when something bad had happened. It's like gratitude was this big joke. It meant to ignore what just happened and focus on something else."

"Hmm," the woman responded, listening. "Sounds like that was pretty frustrating for you."

"Yeah," Robert continued, "it was. The worst was my divorce. I mean, obviously, there was much that led up to it, but to have the finality of it on my birthday was pretty hard."

The woman scooted closer to Robert and put her arm around his shoulders. "Can you tell me what happened?

Robert exhaled deeply, not wanting to talk about the memories, clear and painful in his mind, that he had tried so hard in life to suppress. They sat in silence; Robert's face hidden deep in his hands as he wrestled to find words to describe his experience. Memories pulled at his heart and Robert began to tug at his hair in a similar fashion.

"When I met Mary, I was sure I had found the girl for me," Robert finally started, head down. "She was so full of life and excitement. Her golden hair and ocean blue eyes were enchanting. I could drown in those eyes," Robert laughed bitterly. "I guess I did."

"We met in our oil painting class in New York. She shared the same excitement I had for mixing and matching colors. We would go on walks after class and talk about which paints we would use to match the different colors we could see. So, I was thrilled when she actually took an interest in me. I was shocked because she was always getting looks from every guy around. She could have had any guy she wanted, on any day of the week. I guess that's what she ended up doing anyway," Robert said, clenching his jaws.

"What do you mean?"

"She was always so friendly to everyone. I loved it. It was inspiring to me. I just didn't realize *how* friendly she was," Robert said, tightness closing in on his throat. "After we got married, life seemed like a dream. Sure, it was hard; I mean, we were living in New York, fresh out of grad school and hunting for good jobs to make ends meet. But I felt so rich and full with her in my arms. And then, I got the news."

"What news?"

"That my mother had been diagnosed with breast cancer," Robert said stiffly. "It took the wind out of my sails. She was so young, only forty-seven. Even though I was on the other side of the country, I couldn't imagine this life without her. She had been my rock through so many of the challenges I'd been through as a child. So, I slipped into a depression. Maybe I became more distant, I don't know. But over the next year, while my mom was battling for her life, unbeknownst to me, Mary was seeing other men."

"Oh, Robert," the woman said. She held him tighter, rubbing his back with her warm and gentle hand. "That's awful!"

"It stung deeply. She'd always been so bright and friendly that I couldn't see the flirting for what it was. She was beautiful and men couldn't resist her charm. Finding out was a serious blow to my ego. I couldn't help but wonder if I was good enough for her. Was she unfaithful because my relationship with her wasn't satisfying enough?

"I looked for any sign of real remorse and change in her. I wanted to make it work. I was willing to forgive her and move on. But then, she started to get more honest with me and I learned that it wasn't just a single affair. She had been with multiple men. So, despite the stigma I knew it would create for the both of us, I filed for a divorce. It was one of the hardest things I had done to that point in my life, but I knew I couldn't go on living in the insecurity of my clear inadequacy.

"When I served her the papers, she made a show of wanting to change. She made all kinds of promises, but I had lost trust in anything she said. She didn't want to sign them, I think out of shame, so the process dragged on. I couldn't afford to move out, so we lived together for months in a cold, distant dance. I slept on the couch because I couldn't stand to be in the same bed with her anymore. She finally gave in and the divorce was finalized in November, the day before my birthday. Thanksgiving. The day of gratitude."

"You didn't deserve that, Robert," the woman said. "I'm so sorry you had to go through it all. That must have been terrible."

"It was," Robert replied. He was surprised at how good it felt to hear those words. Friends had said similar things, but it always felt more like token statements meant to fill an awkward moment than to actually empathize with him. Now, he could feel the sincerity of her words and they washed over him.

"What did you do after the divorce?"

"Well, I was a single guy again, just as the Vietnam draft was initiated. I was too old to be drafted, but only by a couple of months. I've always looked younger than my age, so I frequently had people asking me what my draft number was or if I was afraid of being drafted.

"I started to feel a bit paranoid that people were looking at me and thinking that I was dodging the draft in some way. I feared everyone's judgment, even though I knew I wasn't doing anything wrong. So that, on top of being a new divorcee in my twenties, put me in a really dark place."

"I imagine that was pretty scary and lonesome for you," the woman said, her voice soft and caring. "How did you manage?"

"Barely," Robert admitted. "Some days it was everything I could do just to get up and go to work. I could tell I wasn't as careful in some of my conservation work, and that scared me. People would eventually notice and then my career would be over too. That's when Sandra suggested I move out to California and stay with her to let my head clear. Get a change of scenery, you know?

"I decided to do it for two reasons. One, I needed to get away from Mary and the winter gloom of New York. And two, I realized my time to see my mother was running short and I wanted to be close to her."

The woman rested her head on Robert's shoulder. Instinctively, he put his arm around her and held her close. It felt so warm and familiar. His heart burned within him as he felt the transfer of love. It was like medicine for his soul to embrace someone with no need for words to express the love.

"And then you got your job at the museum in L.A., right?" the woman eventually said, prompting him to continue his story.

"Yes. But, like all good things that happen in my life, pain and heartache were hiding in its shadow, waiting to jump out and take it all away," Robert said, coldness returning to his voice.

"But I thought you loved your job at the museum," the woman said, confused. "You said earlier that it was really good for you."

"Oh, it was," Robert said. "It was exactly what I needed at the time. The regular sunshine and warmth of Southern California were good medicine, too. But even there, a dark cloud came and settled over me.

"Not long after I got the job, my mother's health took a turn for the worse. She'd been fighting her cancer so hard. She'd been so optimistic and positive. Each time I visited her I felt like she was doing more to lift my spirits and give me hope than I was doing for her. She would just smile at me with her bright eyes and no eyebrows, bandana wrapped around her bald head. And despite the pain I'm sure she was feeling, she was just radiant.

"But that changed in the spring. The light went out. I could see her pain and she stopped getting out of bed. She was like sand slipping through my fingers, and no matter how hard I tried to hold on, the grains just kept falling out."

The woman didn't say anything. She just held him tighter, urging him to continue.

"I didn't handle the loss very well. The funeral was a blur. Sandra held it together somehow. I was just numb. I needed space, and I figured Sandra and Tom could use some as well. So, I moved out and found my own apartment. I buried myself in my work at the museum to try to fill the hole in my heart that the loss of my mother, and everything else, had created."

Robert felt the woman shaking. As he brought his attention back to her, he realized she was crying. She released her grip on him and turned toward him, putting her hands on his face.

"Oh, Robert. I'm so sorry," she choked out, her warm tears dripping onto Robert's hands. "You went through so much. So much pain. So much heartache. I wanted to take it from you, but I just couldn't. I'm so sorry."

Robert's eyes welled up and breached the levee of his eyelids. A shudder went through his body as tears spilled out onto the woman's hands. Recognition surged upon him in a flood of emotion and tears. Here she was.

"Mom!" Robert wept.

Chapter 10

The Artwork

Spring, 1984

I 've got to pee," Bobby said.

"OK, but hurry. Robert will be here any minute."

Sandra smiled to herself as she watched Bobby awkwardly walk through the front lobby toward the bathroom. That boy was growing up too fast. She couldn't seem to keep him in a pair of shoes for longer than three months.

The information desk was riddled with an array of fliers and maps. She riffled through them absently. She was proud of her brother. He probably had no idea how much inviting Bobby to watch him do a restoration meant to the boy. Robert could be so oblivious, but for some reason, he pulled it together for Bobby. She wondered how Robert would have changed if and his ex-wife had ever had children. He would have been a great dad.

"Where's Bobby?" Robert asked, startling her out of her thoughts. She smiled, hugging him warmly.

"Oh, he had to go to the bathroom," Sandra explained. "He should be back any second now. He's so excited for this. You may not have seen it at the moment, but when you told him he could come watch you do a restoration, he was just giddy inside."

"Giddy?" Robert questioned. "I mean, he smiled a little and said 'sure,' but I wouldn't call that giddy."

"Well, he *is* fourteen now, so I guess that means he's supposed to suppress his emotions and be all apathetic or something," Sandra explained. "He's really not that good at it, but he does put on the teenager mask from time to time. He isn't fooling anyone, though. That's all he's been talking about since you invited him. I get to watch the unveiling of the true colors, he says. And he can't stop smiling. So, thank you for inviting him. It really means a lot to him, and me."

"Well, it'll be fun to share the process with you both," Robert said. He had talked about the process several times in their home, telling the tale as if it were some mystery in a detective novel. And now, they would get to see the colors revealed for themselves.

Bobby walked out of the bathroom, drying his hands off on his faded denim pants. He wore a white, Culture Club t-shirt with a big picture of Boy George plastered to the front of it. A smile stole across his pimpled face the moment he saw Robert.

"Hey, Bobby," Robert greeted the boy. "I almost didn't recognize you with your karma blending into the surroundings like that."

Bobby rolled his eyes. "Funny. Are you going to do that the whole time today?"

"Do what?" Robert asked in mock innocence.

"The bad dad jokes."

"Well, Bobby, someday, when you're as old as I am, your sense of humor will be as refined as mine," Robert said.

"I can't wait," Bobby said, trying to keep a straight face.

"Well," Sandra interrupted. *These boys and their silly banter.* "Shall we go up? I can't wait to see the painting."

The scene as they walked into Robert's office looked like an operating room. The patient, looking a bit worse for wear, lay on a large stainless-steel table. A tray of solutions, cotton swabs, wooden sticks, and even a scalpel lay next to it, perfectly neat and organized.

"I'm excited for you to watch this," Robert said, approaching the table. "Pull up some chairs and I'll explain what we're doing today."

As they gathered on either side of him, Robert inspected the painting like a dutiful physician, looking carefully at the cracks, textures, and tears in the canvas. "You should have seen it before I did the first cleaning. The smoke damage was pretty significant. You could hardly see any color."

"Was it just totally black?" Bobby asked.

"Not totally," Robert explained. "There were portions that were, but it was mostly just smoke grime. It cleaned up fairly well with the washing. The pile of filthy cotton swabs at the end was massive. Now you can see how much smoke was absorbed into the varnish. That's why the whole painting has a dark, acrid tint to it."

"So, what happened to it in the first place?" Bobby asked, observing not just the discoloration, but the big tear as well. Sandra sat back, enjoying Robert in his element and her son soaking up every moment of it.

"This painting went through a lot in its later years. But it had a beautiful life," Robert said, looking fondly at the canvas laying before him. "It was painted by the French artist, Adenet Dupuis. Not much is known about him, but clearly, he was involved in the French Impressionist movement in the 1860s. This painting was done in 1867."

"Wow," Bobby said. "This painting is a hundred and two years older than me!"

"Yep," Sandra smiled, looking fondly at her son. She adored the wonder in his eyes.

"The painting was commissioned by a rich vigneron in France."

"What in the world is a vigneron?" Bobby asked.

"Well, a vigneron is like a husbandman of a vineyard," Robert explained. "He likely had hundreds of acres of grapevines and a villa looking out onto his vineyard. Apparently, he wanted a beautiful painting for his home and asked Mr. Dupuis to create this one. It stayed at the villa for a couple generations, passing from father to son, and was probably enjoyed by many who came to visit the vineyard."

"That sounds so romantic," Sandra said, smiling. She was certain her brother would miss any sort of romanticism involved, but she had to point it out. Maybe it could spark some interest in a social life for him. Maybe he could drop his persistent gloom and see that the sun was shining all around him.

"Sure," Robert dismissed as he began twisting cotton onto sticks to look like large Q-tips. "However, tragedy struck in the early 1900s when a fire broke out at the villa. They'd recently upgraded the lighting in the home to electric lights. There must have been something wrong with the wiring, and it sparked a fire in the main home. Much of the house was burned. Somehow, the painting was rescued during the fire, but not before it experienced extensive smoke damage. The frame had some scorch marks, but luckily the paint wasn't damaged too much from the heat."

"How did it get that big tear in it?" Bobby asked, leaning down, looking closely.

"I'm not a hundred percent sure on that," Robert said. He stacked a pile of the cotton swabs he was making next to the canvas. "My guess is that after it was taken from the home, it was placed in storage with all the undamaged furnishings in the house while the villa was torn down and rebuilt. It probably had a chair or something else fall on it. Either way, it was clearly forgotten, because the painting didn't show up again until fifty or more years later when it was sold at the estate sale for the villa. Some unknowing art collector probably bought it, hoping that it could be restored and was worth something."

Bobby's eyebrows raised as a grin formed on his face. Robert finished rolling the cotton and walked to a cupboard filled with a variety of solutions and chemicals.

"It sat around for several years until just last year when an antique dealer saw it laying in the storehouse of the owner and recognized the textures of the brush strokes as a French Impressionist painting. He encouraged the owner to try to have it restored, figuring it was probably worth a lot of money."

"Is it?" Bobby asked, looking up at Robert.

"That depends on how well I do with the restoration," Robert answered. He tousled Bobby's hair and smiled at the boy. "It's slated to be displayed at the upcoming exhibit in the museum for the Olympics. So you better hope I don't mess it up."

"How do you make sure you don't ruin the painting when you take off the varnish?" Sandra asked. "The chemicals must be pretty strong."

"Good question. That's part of the reason this process is so slow. I have to make sure I have the right chemical compound so only the varnish comes up and none of the paint," Robert explained as he set down a couple bottles of liquid. "Let me show you."

Robert measured and mixed the chemicals into a bowl and dipped one of the huge Q-tips into it. Picking a small, dark corner of the painting, he applied the solution in gentle circles. Dark, yellow smudges began to appear on the stark, white cotton. Robert rotated the swab to maintain a clean surface as he cleaned a two-inch square. In just a minute, what was once nearly black now showed a dark cerulean. Robert paused and sat up.

"Take a look at that!" he said, smiling. It warmed Sandra's heart to see him smile like that. It hadn't been a common sight for years.

Sandra and Bobby leaned off their chairs to look closer at the painting. "Wow," Bobby said, "that's a pretty big difference already."

"And look how clear and rich that color is," Robert beamed. "He's captured the shadows so well." Robert examined his swab carefully and then extended it out to the other two. "You can't see any of that color on the swab, so it looks like I have my cleaning solution just right."

"Did you just guess and get it right?" Sandra asked, looking impressed.

"Well, yes and no. It was an educated guess. I've been doing this for long enough now that I've learned about the different varnishes over the years and which ones were used in which time periods and locations. This isn't the first time I've restored a painting from 1800s France."

"I can see why you love this part," Sandra said, looking closely at the painting again. "The colors really come alive when you remove the varnish."

"Especially when it's been darkened as much as this one," Robert replied. "Now we can continue with the rest of the painting."

"Do you just wash the whole thing?" Bobby asked.

"Yes, but I'll have to do it in sections," Robert answered. "You'll see as I go along. It's a bit of a slow process, but I love it."

Robert dipped another swab into the clear solution and began working in the lower-left corner of the painting. Slowly and methodically, he worked a section of the painting that revealed what appeared to be a rock wall and shrubbery, clearly all in shadow. He then moved across the bottom, sectioning a portion that was the garden path itself. Pockets of sunlight speckled the road in a light saffron hue, a warm and welcoming contrast to the surrounding shadows. The pile of swabs grew as the three talked and marveled at the colors together. When Robert cleared the focal point of the painting, they all sat back and absorbed the beauty of it.

The piece masterfully depicted a beam of light shining through the opening of trees at the top of the painting highlighting a couple walking together on the path. It was simple. The Impressionistic style was loose, but the lights and shadows, laid down in dappled brushstrokes, drew the eye in a captivating and enchanting way.

"What a stunning painting," Sandra commented in a reverent tone. She could see why Robert loved his job so much. The idea of being able to just wipe away the bad on a cotton ball and have all the good to look at probably touched on fantasy for him. If only he could stop focusing on the negative in his life.

"Yeah," Bobby whispered. "I can see why you love your job. You get to be like a time machine."

"That's an interesting way of seeing it," Robert said. "But I guess you're right. I do get to peel back the layers of wear that time has imposed and get a glimpse of what the artist saw when he first painted it. Too bad it has so much damage. You can see where pieces of paint have just come off the canvas entirely. It definitely wasn't handled properly."

"But you can fix it, right?" Bobby asked.

"Of course. It's just that the damage draws so much attention away from the beauty of the painting," Robert said, his face going momentarily dark. "I wonder how Mr. Dupuis would feel looking down on his artwork in such a condition."

"I bet he would be grateful it was in your capable hands," Sandra replied quickly, smiling up at her brother.

Chapter 11

The Accident

October 1996

The bandage over his eye itched. Robert tried to ignore it, but he could feel his heartbeat in the laceration and that kept bringing his attention back to it. It had been a hard day, more eventful than he had wished, and now, he just wanted quiet. Tom had brought him home, and he was glad to be out of the commotion of the hospital. His neck hurt, aches radiating up and down his body, and any light still stabbed at his eyes. So, he lay in his bed with the lights off and unsuccessfully tried to sleep.

Robert worried about Sandra, despite everything she and the doctors had said. He couldn't get the image of her bleeding hands peppered with shards of glass out of his head. The red had been so vibrant and shocking. The panic in her eyes intensified his concern. He couldn't remember much of the accident itself, just flashes of ruby red and amber intensified by the image of Sandra's hands. She had sacrificed her time to help him and had been hurt in doing so. Feelings of guilt pressed upon his chest and flooded his mind.

Other emotions and thoughts began to creep into the periphery of his consciousness. These scared him more, like lurking shadows waiting to jump out at him. Subtly, they inched forward, sliding like ink over the guilt and concern.

Anger.

Blame.

Each attempting to light an unquenchable fire. Robert tried to push these back, rebelling against their irrationality, but they also felt good. He was a victim, again. Misfortune always seemed to find him, and he clenched his teeth at the unfairness of it. These feelings were suffocatingly strong and before too long, he welcomed them. It was easier to feel anger than helplessness, blame than guilt. And so, he stewed in these emotions until he finally drifted into sleep.

When Robert awoke, his eyes burned hot, dry, and scratchy. He lifted his arms to rub at them, but he stopped as the soreness and pain brought the accident fresh into his mind. He groaned, realizing he had forgotten to put in the eye drops before falling asleep. Opening his eyes ignited the fire as sunlight invaded his bedroom. Closing them, Robert sat up, fighting the aches that somehow had intensified in the night.

The eye drops were in the front room on the counter. It seemed so far away now, but he yearned for the relief they could bring. Shuffling like an old man, Robert ventured through his room and out through the hallway, arms out, feeling his way there, only occasionally peeking out to make sure he wouldn't trip over something on the floor. Eventually, he was greeted by the crunch of the white paper bag.

Each drop burned. He struggled with the irritation, blinking and scrunching his eyes as the liquid did its work. Slowly, the fire subsided. With eyes open, Robert could see that the usual blurriness he had lived with for years was gone. A smile tickled at the corners of his mouth. Light still hurt, but hope was creeping in.

He poured himself a tall glass of water, his morning custom, and gingerly sat on his couch. He tried to relax, but stiffness fought each attempt. The phone rang, shattering the silence. Robert jumped at the sound, his heart suddenly racing. Exhaling a long breath, he reached over and picked up the receiver.

"Hello?" Robert answered in a scratchy morning voice.

"Hey Robert, it's Tom," a warm voice greeted him. "Just calling to see how you're doing this morning."

"I'm OK, I guess. A bit sore everywhere, but that's to be expected."

"Yeah, Sandra's pretty sore too."

"How are her hands?" Robert asked. "I couldn't get the picture of them bleeding out of my head last night."

"Surprisingly, they're doing really well. Fortunately, none of the cuts were very deep. There were just a lot of them. Would you like to talk to her?" Robert could hear Sandra in the background telling Tom to give her the phone.

"Yes," Robert answered, and Sandra was on before he even finished.

"Robert, I'm so sorry!" Sandra said, voice sincere and filled with worry. "Are you OK?"

Last night's feelings of victimhood struck him with Sandra's apology. He was surprised by the intensity and darkness of it. "I'll be fine," Robert said, a little coldly, trying to push the feeling away. "How about you?"

"Oh, don't worry about me. How are your eyes?"

Robert looked around his front room. It was still dark, but he could see everything clearly. "They're good. I can read 'Panasonic' on my TV."

"Oh, Robert, that's great!" Sandra breathed out in relief. "So, the blurriness is gone?"

"It seems like it," he returned. "The light still hurts, and the cut over my eye throbs, but as far as I can tell, my vision is good." Reflecting on the positives seemed to keep the darker emotions at bay.

"Well, take it easy. You've got a whole weekend. Let your body recover."

"I know, Sandra. I'm a big boy. My plan is to just lay around in a dark room and do nothing, just like the doctor ordered."

The weekend went slowly. His eyes hurt more than he let on to Sandra. The drops helped some, but there was an aching at the back of his eyes that just wouldn't go away. Robert figured it was likely a headache brewing due to the pain and tension in his neck from the accident. Ibuprofen helped, but not enough to make it go away. So, Robert laid in his bed, eyes closed, listening to classical music on his CD player.

Despite what may have seemed like a relaxing setting, Robert found his mood darkening as the hours went by. Memories of his ex-wife confessing to her affairs crept into his mind. He had been devastated at the betrayal; depression leached his life and energy. Much like now, Robert had locked himself in his room, lights off, confined to the bed. Little would coax him out. The darkness had wrapped him up in a deep suffocating blanket. Only the threat of losing his job pulled at him hard enough to escape the bed. Art had always been his escape from the darkness, the colors sparking life and excitement back into motion. But the thrill of the artwork had faded too.

Feeling the pull of that darkness, Robert did what he could to fight the magnetic heaviness of old regrets, pains, and resentments. He took the classical CD out of the player and replaced it with *Abbey Road* by The Beatles. The familiar weepy tones of the electric guitar brought a quick smile to his face. Track by track he reveled in the genius of the iconic band. And then, George Harrison's voice serenaded the words, "I don't want to leave her now." The beautiful ballad of "Something," despite its message of unity and love with a spouse, pulled him back to the divorce.

"Bah," Robert shouted to no one as he got up and removed the CD. Looking through his CDs for something different, he noticed a black speck floating around his vision just outside the center of his focus. In an attempt to wipe it away, he rubbed his eye, irritating it further. The spot remained. *How did a bug get in my eye?* he thought.

The bathroom mirror didn't help much. He couldn't see anything in his eye, and the light still hurt. So, figuring that whatever was stuck in his eye would work its way out on its own, Robert returned to his room to rest his eyes more.

Knocking. Slowly, Robert's consciousness emerged out of a fuzziness. The knock came again. Opening his eyes, he felt the familiar burn. He groaned as he realized that, once again, he had forgotten to put in the eye drops before going to bed. More persistently now, the knocking continued.

"Robert?" a muffled voice came, "Are you OK?"

Robert looked at his alarm clock to see the red numbers shining out at him through the dark room: 10:23 am. A little confused and stiff, he pulled himself out of bed to answer the door. He stumbled through the darkness, squinting back the dryness of his eyes and the brightness of the hallway outside his room. Finally opening the door, Robert was greeted with the shocked faces of Tom and Sandra. Tom held a couple of plastic grocery bags in his hand.

"You look terrible," Sandra said.

"Well, thank you," Robert grumbled.

"Have you changed your clothes at all?" She looked him up and down, noticing the wrinkled and disheveled shirt and pants. The bandage above his eye was a little crusty with brown blood peeking through the outside.

"I fell asleep with my clothes on yesterday," Robert explained as he walked back into his kitchen, the two following behind him. "Your knocking woke me up. I must have needed the rest."

"Well, we brought you breakfast," Tom smiled, setting the bags down on the counter. "Nothing like a healthy breakfast to get that body healing quickly."

"That's kind of you," Robert muttered as he looked for his eye drops. He finally found them by the CD player and remembered why he had gone to bed early. A few more specks floated through his vision as he scanned the room. He put drops in each eye, hoping this would wash out whatever was stuck in there.

"How are your eyes doing this morning?" Sandra asked, watching him closely.

"They burn," he said automatically. "And I seem to keep getting stuff stuck inside them."

"What do you mean, stuff?" Tom asked.

"I just keep having these spots float around in my vision," Robert explained. "I've looked at my eyes for bugs or eyelashes, but there isn't anything there."

"Can you see the spots now?" Sandra asked.

Robert looked around the room at the white walls and could see four or five specks move around with the movement of his eyes. "Yes," he answered.

"Let me look," Sandra said. Her gauzed hands pressed awkwardly on his face as she peered into each eye. "Look left." He complied. "Now right."

"Do you see anything?" Robert asked.

"Well, they're still pretty red, but I can't see anything else. How long has this been going on?"

"I noticed it yesterday, but I've been keeping everything pretty dark, so who knows."

"Doesn't seem normal to me," Tom commented as he pulled bagels, cream cheese, and orange juice out of the bags.

"Have you told the doctors about this?" Sandra asked.

"Sandra, I just woke up. How could I have told the doctors?" Robert said defensively.

"I'm just saying, you should ask if this is common or not. I can't imagine you'd want these floaties in your vision while you're restoring artwork."

Robert exhaled and shook his head. "I have a follow-up appointment tomorrow. I'll talk to them about it then. They're probably not even in the office today."

Sandra gave Robert a long look. Then, seemingly satisfied, she sat down at the table. "Tom, can you spread some strawberry cream cheese on one of these bagels for me? This gauze really gets in the way."

They sat and ate in casual conversation, sunlight streaming in through the windows as the sun rose in the sky. Tom doted on them, Sandra with her bandaged hands, and Robert keeping his eyes closed as much as possible.

"When do you go back to work, Robert?" Tom asked.

"Tuesday," he answered. "I gave the weekend a buffer day just in case."

"That was smart," Tom said as he washed a bagel down with a swallow of juice.

"Yeah, well, now I just hope my neck isn't too stiff," Robert said as he rubbed his neck.

"Are you working on any projects right now?" Tom asked through another bite of bagel.

"I've got a couple pieces that I'm working on from a client that had some amateur try to restore. They look terrible. You can clearly see all the repairs, if you can even call them that. Bobby could have done just as good of a restoration without any training. So, I'll have to try to strip them down to the original painting. I just hope they didn't paint directly on the original."

"What do you mean?" asked Tom. "Of course they painted on the original."

"Well, yes and no," Robert explained. "A trained conservator will put a coat of varnish down once a painting has been cleaned and repaired. That way, when they do the touch-up paint, it's easy to remove any non-original conservation work. It keeps a layer between the original artist's painting and anything added afterward."

"That's smart," Tom replied.

"How long will that take?" Sandra asked.

"That depends entirely on what I find as I clean the painting. It could be a week; it could be a month."

"Well," Tom said, picking up the trash from the table, "good luck with that."

"Thanks," Robert returned, standing to help Tom.

While Robert was appreciative of the gesture of breakfast and the company, he was eager to be alone again. He didn't have to keep up pretenses with himself. If he felt irritable, he could be irritable. If he felt sad, he could cry. He didn't have to be strong. So, he went through the motions of smiles and hugs as Sandra and Tom left. He thanked them and assured them that he would be OK. He promised Sandra he would talk to the doctor about the spots in his vision. Tomorrow. For now, he would go back to bed. In the dark.

He slept easily. He wasn't sure for how long, but when he woke, everything was profoundly dark. There must have been a power outage because even the light from his alarm was dark. Sitting up in the pitch black, Robert shuffled through his room, trying to find his way to the door. Finding the wall, he inched his way to the light switch and flipped it up and down. Nothing. The power was out.

He walked out in the main room, hoping to get at least some light from the moon shining through the windows, but the darkness remained absolute. Robert waved his hand in front of his face. Nothing. *It can't be* this *dark,* he thought. He felt his way to the phone, knocking many things over in the process. Robert awkwardly felt for the buttons, straining to remember the ordering of numbers, and dialed Sandra's home.

"Hello?" Sandra's happy voice greeted him on the other end. Robert was surprised that her voice was so happy in the middle of the night. He was sure he would have woken her.

"Hey, Sandra, sorry to call so late. Is your power out too?"

"It's not *that* late," Sandra said with some mockery in her tone. "Our power is fine. How long has yours been out?"

"I'm not sure. I woke up and everything was dark. I can't see a thing in my house."

"Nothing?" Sandra sounded worried.

"No," Robert repeated. "It's pitch black."

"Robert," her voice was suddenly serious. "It's 1:15 in the afternoon. You should be able to see just fine."

Chapter 12

The Accident

October 1996

I

t appears that you have a serious case of retinal detachment," a gruff voice pronounced with finality.

"What does that mean?" Robert asked, feeling a deep dread spread throughout his body.

"Your retina lines the back wall of your eye and is responsible for collecting light and transferring that into an electrical signal for your brain. Think of it like the film in a camera. It captures the image," the doctor methodically explained. "Your retina has pulled off your eye and is allowing fluid to pass under it. This likely happened at the time of your accident. Unfortunately, this separation has damaged the blood flow to your retina, causing significant damage."

"What is the procedure to fix it and how long is the recovery?" Robert asked, his heart starting to pump more rapidly.

There was a long pause followed by a deep breath. "Normally, we would do one of several procedures to pull or push the retina back onto the eye until it can reattach itself."

"What do you mean, 'normally'?" Robert asked, feeling worry and irritation rise in his chest.

"Most patients come having complaints with their vision, but rarely blindness. Things like tunnel vision or floaties are the most common. We're able to act quickly in those situations to correct the problem. However, once full blindness sets in, there's little chance of the vision being recovered."

He was so matter-of-fact. The lack of emotion stung almost as much as the words themselves. "Are you saying there's nothing you can do? That I'm blind? How is that possible? I could see just fine this morning," Robert's words were rushing out of his mouth.

"There are some things we could try, but the chances for success are really low," the doctor said slowly. "The progression of your symptoms seems to have been very quick. Typically, it would take several days for someone to experience symptoms like yours now. Early intervention is the key."

"So, can we try those things now? I need my eyes, they're my livelihood. We have to try," Robert was pleading now. He felt a hand rest on his arm, and he flinched. Sandra had been so quiet that he almost forgot she was there with him. Her gauzed fingers squeezed his forearm and calmed him for a moment.

"You've been scheduled for an emergency procedure already. It might be a couple of hours for our surgical team to gather and prepare," the doctor said. "Working around your recent LASIK surgery may be challenging. A nurse will be by shortly to bring you the paperwork."

Robert's whole body slumped in his chair. A sharp pain in his neck forced him to sit back up. He felt defeated. Tears welled in his eyes and his throat tightened, making it difficult to breathe. Leaning his head against the wall, Robert wrapped his arm over his eyes attempting to hide his emotion.

Sandra rubbed his knee, not knowing what to say and sensing that things were not going to be OK. They sat in silence until the nurse arrived with a clipboard of papers to sign. Awkwardly, she explained the content of each page and where Robert would need to write his signature.

"I can't see," Robert exclaimed. "How am I supposed to sign anything?"

"Robert!" Sandra said, squeezing his knee. "Be nice. She's just doing her job." She turned back to the nurse apologetically and explained in a quiet voice, "He's totally blind right now. But I'll take care of it."

"I'm sorry, I didn't mean…" the nurse drifted off looking back and forth between the two.

"It's OK, he's just understandably upset," Sandra explained, and the nurse walked off.

The tension accented the silence. Robert was taking deep, slow breaths, clearly trying to calm down. Sandra stared at him, sorting through the flood of thoughts and emotions she was feeling and trying to fathom what was going through Robert's mind.

Cautiously, Sandra began, "I think I could guide your hand to the right spot on each page to sign."

Robert didn't respond. He just continued to breathe; eyes covered. Sandra placed the clipboard in his lap and placed the pen in his right hand. He flinched a little as she did so but didn't reject it.

"I know this is hard, Robert, but I'm trying to help," she said. "There are only about three places you have to sign."

Slowly, he moved his hand to the top of the papers. "Where do I sign?" he whispered.

Sandra moved his hand so the pen touched the line with the first X. Robert scribbled a signature just below the line that sloped down into the writing below. "Good," Sandra lied. "That looks great. No problem."

Robert slowly came to awareness. He was lying in a bed. Distant conversations droned on, mostly female voices. Opening his eyes to try to get his bearings, Robert realized they were both covered in some sort of gauze. It all came flooding back. The surgery. The accident. The blindness. He started to cry.

"He's waking up," a familiar voice called out. "Nurse? I think he's coming to," the voice faded as footsteps carried the sound away to wherever the nurse was. And then Sandra was back, right at his side. "Robert, how are you feeling?"

"Blind," the word struggled out through an emotion-filled throat.

Sandra's bandaged fingers grabbed his hand in response. Words seemed useless, and she didn't know what to say anyway, so she just squeezed his hand, thankful he couldn't see the tears slipping down her cheeks.

*****

"He can stay in Bobby's old room," Tom whispered as the doctors talked with Robert. "We'll make it work."

Sandra's heart was breaking. Guilt crushed down upon her from every angle as she watched her brother's world fall apart. *Why Robert? Why now?* The questions stoked her anxiety. *Why did I suggest the surgery? How will he ever forgive me?*

"Thank you," Sandra choked out. "I feel terrible. He keeps telling me that he's lost everything. He's worse than after the divorce. Any hope and light he had is just gone."

"We'll just keep him close like last time," Tom said. She stared up at him stoically watching the nurses tend to Robert. "We'll make it work."

"I can't imagine what he's going through right now. His eyes! Why did it have to be his eyes?" Mascara bled down Sandra's cheeks. She absently wiped the tears away smearing dark smudges around her eyes. "The only thing that pulled him out of his depression then was his restoration work and his love of color. I can't think of anything that will pull him out anymore."

"We'll figure it out, Sandra," Tom answered, pulling her in under his arm and holding her close. "We'll figure it out."

They stood on the outer edge of the room watching Robert and listening to the doctors and nurses talking, wondering if he was even listening. The bandages across his eyes masked any emotion. He could have been sleeping and they wouldn't have known. And yet the doctors continued.

Then, surprising them, Robert spoke out clearly. "When can I take these bandages off? They aren't really doing anything."

Sandra groaned. She could almost see the spark snuffed out. The callousness was taking over. She bit her lip to stop herself from trying to say something positive. He would hear it anyway.

"They're there to prevent any infection after the surgery," the doctor explained. "The dressing will need to be changed tomorrow, but it should be fine after a day or two."

"But the surgery didn't work, so why does it even matter?"

"We're not 100% certain it didn't work, but either way, an infection could cause bigger problems," the doctor explained.

"Bigger than me being blind?" Robert's tone was flat, though lined with cynicism.

"Yes," the doctor replied, ignoring Robert's attitude. "Infections can spread and create big problems. Especially when they are around the inside of your head."

Robert went quiet again, but Sandra could tell the seed of bitterness had been planted. She had seen it before.

The doctor approached Tom and her with a concerned look on his face. "We're going to keep him overnight for observations," he said, and then, lowering his voice, continued. "It's very unlikely that the surgery made any difference. The circulation to his retinas was gone. It would take a miracle for them to reattach now." Returning to his regular volume he added, "Does he have anyone at home that will be able to watch over him?"

"He'll move in with us," Tom said quickly.

"Ok," the doctor seemed pleased. "He'll need a lot of support at first. I'll have the nurse bring you some resource materials so you can access different accommodations and supports. Do you have any questions?"

They shook their heads in unison and then watched the doctors and nurses file out of the room. Sandra sat down in the navy-blue chair at the side of the bed and reached for Robert's hand.

"Robert," she started softly, "Tom and I have been talking, and we decided that you can stay at our house as long as you need. You can have Bobby's room right next to the bathroom."

"Thank you," Robert whispered, turning his back to Sandra, ending the conversation.

Chapter 13

The Artwork

Spring, 1984

I've got to fill the gaps," Robert explained. "You can't restore the picture with chunks of the painting missing. Well, I guess you could, but it wouldn't technically be a restoration, would it?"

Sandra and Bobby smiled as they watched Robert scoop pale putty onto a palette knife and scrape it into the holes of missing paint. They had been with him all afternoon watching him repair the painting. Fixing the tear had been like watching a surgeon carefully graft and stitch a gaping wound. He made it look easy, though it was so meticulous: cutting and pasting individual canvas fibers to cross the gap, cutting exact shapes of canvas to fill holes; it was clear he had done this several times, and they were fascinated by the process.

"The hard thing about restoring an Impressionistic painting is getting the texture right," Robert explained as he worked with the putty. "You can see how the brush strokes vary in how thick and thin the paint is applied. In a way, it's almost like large stippling. Think about Monet's *Water Lily Pond* or Van Gogh's *Starry Night*; each is a collection of thick strokes of paint laid out in patterns and colors that capture the eye. It's one of the things I love about the Impressionist movement. But," Robert paused as he looked closer at the canvas, feeling the surface with his fingers, "It makes for a challenge in creating a seamless look with each brushstroke."

"Wow," Bobby said, "that's crazy. Do you ever just give up on the process and say it's good enough?"

Robert laughed as he scanned the painting for gaps or holes in the paint. "That's tempting sometimes. However, when you're really invested in something, for one reason or another, you want to see it through to the end," Robert stood up and turned to look directly at Bobby. "I feel an obligation, or a commitment, to both the original artist and the painting, to bring it back to how it was intended to be. Art isn't created for itself. It's meant to be enjoyed and experienced by others. The more fully I can restore it to its original state, the better the artwork can fulfill its purpose in being created."

"That's really philosophical," Bobby teased.

"Well, when you spend hours by yourself in a room with a painting every day, you end up doing a lot of thinking," Robert explained, returning his attention to the painting.

"When do you start adding the color?" Sandra asked as she looked at her watch.

"*Matching* the color," Robert corrected. "Probably not till tomorrow. The putty will need to be cleaned up and dry before I can start on that. It's a pretty long process." He looked up at Sandra. "Why do you ask? Getting bored yet?"

"Well, it *is* pretty riveting," Sandra said sarcastically. "But I don't think dinner is going to make itself."

Robert looked up at the digital clock on his shelf glowing the red numbers 5:14. "Dang, time always goes too fast." He stood and stretched his back. "Thanks for coming. It's nice to have someone here to talk with while I do this."

"Any time, old man," Bobby teased. "Thanks for letting us come. It's really rad watching you do your work."

"Rad?" Robert mocked.

Bobby rolled his eyes. "Sorry, I mean, It was really swell. Your job is the cat's meow."

They laughed at each other as Robert started putting away tools. "Respect your elders, you little whipper-snapper."

"Do you want to have dinner with us tonight?" Sandra interrupted the banter.

"Oh, you don't need to do that Sandra," Robert replied as he picked up his tools and walked across the room to put them away.

"It'd be nice to have you over, and you wouldn't have to make something for yourself," she pressed.

"I wasn't planning on making my dinner. I figured I would have some greasy teenager at McDonald's do that for me," Robert returned.

"I could let Bobby make dinner if you're really wanting something prepared by a greasy teenager."

"Mom!" Bobby complained.

"I love you dear, but apparently your uncle has an affinity for the culinary masterpieces of the young, novice chefs. You have to please the masses—or Robert—in this instance."

"Well, when you put it that way," Robert chuckled, "how could I possibly resist?"

"Are you dating anyone, Robert?" Sandra asked as they sat around the kitchen table eating the Hamburger Helper she had helped Bobby make. Bobby was busy shoveling spoonfuls into his mouth as Tom stared him down with the where-are-your-table-manners-when-we-have-a-guest look.

"It's a trap!" Robert muttered in his best Admiral Akbar impersonation. Bobby choked on noodles, trying to stifle a laugh, and ended up in a coughing fit. Flecks of food sprayed out onto his plate and the table.

"Bobby! Cover your mouth!" Tom said sternly as he stood and walked across the kitchen to grab some paper towels.

"Are you OK, Bobby?" Sandra asked.

"I'm fine, Mom," Bobby answered. He took the paper towels from his dad and wiped the table around his plate before wiping his nose and face. "You almost got noodles out my nose with that one, Robert."

"Sorry, bud," Robert stated with false seriousness. "You just never know when you'll have to apply evasive maneuvers. I should have known your mom would lure me in to probe about my social life."

"That's not what I was doing!" Sandra said in surprise. "I was just making conversation."

"Mm-hmm," Robert raised his eyebrow at her.

"And now I'm more curious as to why you're avoiding the question," Sandra stared back at him.

"Well, if you must know, I am *not* dating anyone. I'm still the lonely, old curmudgeon I was the last time you asked."

"Any prospects?" Sandra asked.

"So, it's to be an interrogation," Robert sidestepped. He was tired of people thinking that his happiness depended on whether or not he was in a relationship with someone. Relationships like that had been the source of his unhappiness, so why would another make him happy?

"What about that nice lady at the museum?" Sandra continued, ignoring the snide comment. "You know, the one with the glasses?"

"Sandra, there are lots of ladies at the museum who wear glasses."

"Oh, you know what I mean," Sandra said in exasperation. "She was the one that probably told you we were at the museum today. She had on the khaki skirt and white blouse."

Robert remembered. He couldn't remember how long she had been working there, but long enough to know she had been friendly on several occasions. She also had a pleasant smile. Realizing he couldn't remember her name sparked his memory that he was going to try to get Sandra to find it out for him.

"I think I know who you're talking about," Robert said.

"You should ask her out," Sandra smiled.

"I don't know her name though," Robert grimaced.

"So, ask her."

"At this point, it would just be awkward," Robert started. "She's been working with me for a long time and always says my name. To ask hers would just scream that I don't care enough to remember her."

"Or that you're a lonely, old curmudgeon," Tom winked at Robert as he picked up his empty plate and carried it to the sink.

"Neither of which is very attractive," Robert continued good-naturedly. "Maybe you could find it out for me, Sandra. Isn't that what you want anyway?"

"Of course I'll help you, big brother," Sandra said. She smiled at him looking proud of herself. "Would you also like me to give her a note and have her check yes, no, or maybe to see if she likes you?"

Robert laughed. "An interrogation and public humiliation. Your tactics are ruthless, Sandra."

Chapter 14

The Afterlife

W hy didn't you tell me it was you?" Robert asked, choking back tears.

"You had to figure it out yourself, Robert," his mother whispered, wiping tears from his cheek. "Healing is a process of self-discovery. I can help, but I can't do it for you."

"What do you mean?"

"Healing in heaven isn't much different than healing in life," she explained. "It isn't magic. Most people come expecting all the bad things to just be gone. We all want the easy way out. We want the mistakes and accidents and trials to just be erased from our history. But it doesn't work that way, and I've come to be very grateful that it doesn't."

"But that's not what you taught me, Mom," Robert slumped. "You taught me about a restoration—that everything would be restored to its perfect state."

"And it will," his mother smiled and held his hands in hers. "You are an art restorer. You should understand this better than anyone else."

"That's different."

"No, it isn't, Robert. You are a beautiful work of art. There's no magic wand here. You have imperfections and pains that need to be repaired. That isn't going to happen just because you died. You're going to have to put in the work. Right now, you're just paying attention to the damage and imperfections," she squeezed his hands, "so you can't see the beautiful masterpiece of your life."

Robert's head dropped. "My life was not a masterpiece. It was an incomplete painting."

"And *that* is why you are still blind in heaven."

He snapped up, staring in the general direction of his mother's voice. "What? I'm blind now because my life was incomplete?"

"No. You're blind because you refuse to recognize that there was more to your life than just pain and misfortune."

"Oh, so you're saying it's my fault I'm blind here?" Robert spat.

"Yes," she answered firmly. "Your physical blindness in life was clearly an accident, and a heartbreaking one at that. But the real tragedy was your refusal to see all the good and beauty around you after that. Your blindness started long before the accident."

Robert shook his head, shocked at what his mother was saying. She had never been this bold in life. Where was the comfort and understanding? This…this was different. His blindness was his fault? How could that be possible?

"I've told you several times now, sight is so much more than vision. Sight is a choice; vision is a blessing. So perhaps, right now, your blindness is a gift.

"How can you say that Mom?" Robert said, letting go of her hands. "My blindness was the greatest curse of my life."

"Yes, it was," she said knowingly, taking his hands again. "And in Heaven, it has woken you to a reality you couldn't, or wouldn't, see in life. Had your vision been restored, without your sight, you would never have been able to fully enjoy heaven, just like you weren't able to fully enjoy life."

They sat in silence for what seemed to Robert like hours. His mind battled against her words. It couldn't be true. But how could the person he trusted the most in life be lying to him in Heaven? His life had been a constant barrage of misfortune, betrayal, judgment, and loss. He saw all of that in fine detail. It had painted his world and shaped who he had become. How could she say he didn't see things? He saw, clearly, what others couldn't.

"Robert," his mother broke the silence, "your focus on the negatives in life prevented you from seeing the full spectrum of color. You were looking through a filter."

"A filter?" Robert shouted, surprised at such a shocking turn of emotions. "This is ridiculous, Mom. How can you say that?"

Robert stood, stumbling and tripping through the unfamiliar environment; emotions too flooded to care. Tall grass slapped defensively at his knees as he marched aimlessly through the underbrush. Each step presented new obstacles pushing him back, hindering his retreat. He growled at the stones and branches waving his arms erratically. Rose bushes met his hands with thorns angry at his insensitivity. The sharp daggers stoked his frustration as he pulled back, lost and nursing their bites.

"You're doing it right now," his mother's voice whispered, suddenly at his side.

"Doing what?"

"What you did in life," she said, calmly sliding her hand around his elbow.

"Stumbling around and getting hurt because I'm blind?" Robert retorted.

"That's part of it, though I think we're talking about different kinds of blindness," she carefully walked him away from the thorn bushes and into a clearing.

"Then what's the other part?" Robert asked, calming a bit.

"For so much of your life, you had people around you who cared deeply for you. They served and supported you, but you missed it. You chose to focus on your sadness—your resentment and misfortunes. You focused on the negative things that were there, and they were, but that was all you could see. If you were hurt in some way, you ignored the love around you and stumbled off only to get hurt more."

Robert was quiet again. His mother's gentle touch had calmed him. They sat back down and just held hands. He didn't know how to process what she was telling him. Waves of emotion crashed and receded against his consciousness as he reflected on the difficulties of his life. Regretfully, he had to admit that he couldn't see any of the good she was talking about. It was just sadness and resentment and darkness.

"So, you're saying I'm blind now because of what I couldn't see in life?" Robert asked.

"Yes," she answered matter-of-factly. "Though it isn't that you didn't have the ability to see it—more that you wouldn't. And as a result, you're missing the whole picture. When you look at your life, you have holes and cracks where you missed the love and service and goodness that were always around you. So, you say your life was incomplete, but that is where you're wrong. Your life was complete. And it was beautiful. But your focus on the negative, the misfortune, prevented you from seeing it. That neglect is what heightened the damage and left your experience darkened and faded."

Robert's mind was reeling. He reflected on the hundreds of paintings he had restored before his blindness. His mother's language pricked his heart and challenged the paradigm of his life. But he didn't understand or know what to do with the new perspective. He felt himself getting overwhelmed—head getting hot and mental energy slipping away. He laid down, the grass feeling cool against his skin.

"So, what do I do?" Robert pleaded. "I don't have any memory of the good you're referring to. How can I see again if what I need to do is to see the things I can't see?"

"Robert, you're an art restorer. You know the process."

"Mom, this is different. This is my life, not some two-dimensional painting."

"It isn't that much different, son. And you know the process."

Chapter 15

The Artwork

April 1984

It wasn't that hard, Robert," Sandra said as she handed him a brown bag lunch, much like the ones that their mother would hand them each day before sending them off for school. "She had an identification badge hanging around her neck."

"And?" Robert probed, not looking up from the painting.

"And what?" Sandra was annoyed at Robert's seeming indifference.

He continued inspecting the painting to make sure he had filled the gaps before he could begin painting. "Her name. What is it?"

"Heather," she said flatly. "Are you even going to try, Robert?"

"Try what?" he asked, finally looking up.

"To pay attention. To notice other people and care about something other than your work."

"Whoa, settle down," Robert said, surprised at her accusation. "This was your idea, remember?"

"You asked me to find out her name. I did. Was that just because you were too lazy and uncaring to look up and see her nametag? I mean, seriously Robert, it's not that hard to make relationships."

"Sandra, a guilt trip isn't going to motivate me," he retorted. "I don't know if you remember or not, but my last relationship wasn't exactly a pleasant experience."

"Robert, that was *fifteen years* ago. Don't you think it's time to move on?"

He didn't answer. Looking back down at the painting, he took some deep breaths and tried to settle himself. People didn't understand what he had gone through and the betrayal that still gripped at his sense of self. He wasn't mad at Sandra, but she kept pushing on old wounds. He wanted to be left alone. Artwork wouldn't betray him. Colors could easily be matched and restored. But love, and excitement of being in love? That was gone. Those colors were false; seen through rose-colored glasses and rooted in ignorance. You can't restore something that wasn't true in the first place.

"I'm sorry, Robert," Sandra said softly as she walked to the door. "Maybe I'm too pushy. I just hate seeing you sad and stuck in the past. You deserve to be happy." She paused halfway out the door. "I thought of a way you could remember her name, for what it's worth. Heather is a pinkish-purple flower. Similar to the ones on the painting you're working on right now."

The door closed. He winced at the click of metal but didn't look up. His eyes were focused on the purple flowers in *The Garden Path*.

Chapter 16

The Afterlife

Can you tell me what I wasn't paying attention to? I mean, a painting can't restore itself."

"Before I do, I have some questions you need to ask yourself," she positioned herself directly in front of Robert and held his hands in hers. "What are three things you were most grateful for in life?"

Robert faltered. Each time he thought of something his mind jumped to some way it was taken from him or a negative component of it. He wanted to mention his time in art school and learning about colors, but it only brought up memories of Mary. Her beautiful, smiling face peeked into his consciousness, and like a knife to the heart, all he could see was betrayal.

"You're thinking too hard, Robert," his mother said.

"But how can I be grateful for stuff that ended up hurting me?"

"That isn't what I am asking right now. Just share something you're grateful for. You don't need to pick each thing up and examine it for any bad spots. Just be present and don't overthink it."

"Fine," he said, frustrated with himself. "Like I said earlier; color. I'm grateful for color. But I lost that…"

"No buts," his mother interrupted. "Stay with gratitude."

"It's just difficult to be grateful for something I loved and lost."

"You didn't lose colors, Robert," she said firmly.

"Yes, I did," Robert retorted. "I lost the ability to see one of the things I loved most in life."

"Only with your eyes."

"What?" Robert sputtered, confused and defensive.

"Robert?" his mother calmly probed.

"What?"

"When I had you lay down a few moments ago and pay attention to your other senses, what did you *see* while you were feeling the grass and dirt?"

For a moment, he hesitated, ready to tell her that he couldn't see anything. That he was blind. And then, he realized it. He had seen. He had seen dancing blades of grass, dressed in rich tones of green. He could see the darkness of the wet, fertile soil between his fingers. He hadn't seen it with his eyes, obviously, but there it had been, clearly in his mind, just as if he had.

A gust of wind blew, rustling the leaves of the tree that they were sitting under. Sunlight danced through the gaps in the leaves, shining random patterns of light across his face. He could feel the warmth in pockets on his face, and the orange glow illuminating his eyelids.

"I saw the memory of color," Robert admitted.

"And yet, it wasn't a memory, was it?" she pushed.

"What do you mean?"

"You hadn't seen that grass or dirt before," she explained. "You created something new and beautiful in your mind based on your experiences with the past. That is how we will need to fill the gaps. You can reframe your past by changing the way you think about it. You keep telling yourself that everything was bad, but it wasn't. That's just what you chose to focus on, and so your memories are filled with negatives. There was good in your life, Robert. Change your view. Fill the gaps by changing your focus."

Chapter 17

The Accident

November 1996

W ould you like me to stay longer?" Sandra asked. "Or I could see if Bobby could come over and stay the night with you."

"No," Robert replied. "That's kind of you, but I need to figure this out. I can't depend on others to be my eyes for the rest of my life."

"Are you sure? It won't be a problem," Sandra couldn't keep the worry out of her voice. "I mean, at least wait until after the holidays, and your birthday."

"I'm fine, Sandra," Robert repeated, irritation starting to bubble up.

He wasn't fine. Fine was when there weren't any problems, or that they were so insignificant that they never crept into your active consciousness. But this, this new state of being, how could it ever be fine? The sun had gone out. Lights had been extinguished everywhere. Colors had retreated, hiding in front of his face, never to reveal themselves again. He was not fine.

"Ok, but if you need anything, please call," Sandra said.

"I will," Robert lied.

Robert had spent the first month of blindness living at his sister's home. He had needed the help. The simple, everyday tasks had been so much harder. Walking, going to the bathroom, eating. He hadn't realized how much he had relied on his eyes. And now, his eyes betrayed him. They no longer blessed him with beautiful glimpses of the world outside of his head. Closed windows, shutters nailed tight, without a crack of light to illuminate the lonely room.

His heart twisted and ached, but he kept it all inside, needing to appear resilient for Sandra. As much as the resentment, bitterness, and sadness tried to wash over him and drag him down, he couldn't let her see it. He didn't want to add to her guilt and worry. He loved her too much for that. But he also knew the tension that his presence in their home was creating. He could hear them at night, talking loudly behind closed doors. He couldn't hear all the words, but he could feel the meaning behind the tone. He was a burden. He couldn't do that to them. Couldn't let his misfortune pull apart their perfect relationship.

Sandra walked out the front door of his small home. He sat and listened to the car door shut, the engine start, followed by the annoying squealing of her fan belt, and then the eventual silence that let him know he was truly alone. He sat there for what seemed like hours. He had no idea what time it was. He couldn't see any clocks. Eventually, his bladder told him he needed to get up.

He had been to the bathroom hundreds, if not thousands of times before. He knew precisely where it was in relation to the couch he stood up from. But now, somehow this felt like a game of Marco Polo, only the bathroom wasn't yelling back "Polo" for him. Arms outstretched, Robert shuffled toward the commode, searching for the walls to guide him along the way.

Hands touching the wall, he walked more confidently now, eager to relieve himself. Suddenly, his hand hit the frame of a painting, knocking it askew. It was one of his favorites. He had found it in a gallery years ago, shining in brilliant colors, almost calling to him. He had stood in front of it for several minutes as others walked past and around him, unnoticed. It was an African scene, with women walking along a road, baskets balanced on their heads, dressed in vibrant clothing. He loved the contrast of reds and greens, yellows and purples, blues and oranges, each subtly done with thick brushstrokes to create a full texture.

And now, here it was, unseen and lopsided on his wall. He attempted to straighten it before he realized he wouldn't be able to see if it was level. Emotion began to build deep from his gut. Like someone pouring too quickly into a small glass, Robert felt the shudders of a sob, hearing the cry from his lips before he could resist the emotion. In an effort to hold back the tide of sadness, anger rushed to his aid. He grabbed the frame in both hands and held it in front of his unseeing eyes. He screamed at it, a loud, animalistic shout.

"Why!? Why did you take away the only thing that really mattered?" He shook the painting like a poor, innocent child. "Why is it that everything good in my life is ripped away from me? Can't I just keep one thing that brings me joy? Is that too much to ask?"

The painting didn't respond, and the blackness would have drowned out any response if it tried. He punched the wall the painting had been pulled from and felt the drywall give way to his attack. His knuckles throbbed a little, bringing him back to the moment and the painting tensely hanging from his other hand.

Shaking his head at his outburst, Robert reached out to the wall to feel for the nail the painting had hung from. The punch left a fist-sized hole in the wall that Sandra would surely question him about. He pushed aside that irritation as his hand swept up and around, feeling the textured surface but finding no nail.

"This would be a lot easier if I could see," Robert muttered to the hallway. The pressure from his bladder inflamed his frustration as he moved up and down the hallway, trying to find the missing nail, running into other paintings in the process. His anger reached a crescendo of frustration and exasperation and he threw the painting down the hallway. The sickening snap of wood extinguished the flame of anger, bringing a fresh tidal wave to wash over him. He dropped to his knees unable to stand against the multitude of emotions. He sat, hands over his face, and sobbed deep, drowning tears.

Chapter 18

The Afterlife

Let's start by understanding that things in your life weren't *taken* from you."

Robert's eyebrows shot up. She was goading him again. "How can you say that? My sight was taken from me," Robert said, incredulously.

"No, Robert. Again, your sight was your own doing. Your vision is another matter," she corrected. "Losing your vision was exceptionally unfortunate, but it was lost, not taken."

"That's just semantics, Mom."

"No, Robert. It's an important distinction, and it will be important in helping you to fill the gaps in your memory and perspective of life."

"I can't see how that can be all that important," Robert fumed. "Simply 'looking at the bright side' doesn't change what happened, Mom. Taken. Lost. What does it matter? Either way, it was gone." Robert turned away from his mother. "And it's still gone," he muttered through clenched teeth.

"Who took your vision away from you?" she challenged.

"What?"

"You claim it was taken from you. Who took it?" Her tone was firm but calm.

Robert stewed over the question. He wanted to find blame, something to prove he was right. The familiar darkness crept into the corners of his consciousness. It pushed his heart toward a familiar target. Part of him knew it wasn't fair, but he needed a target for his emotions.

"Are you noticing your thoughts?" she prodded. "What are you focused on? Are you really seeking for understanding or are you clinging to a singular perspective? Who took your vision?"

"Life took it away!" Robert shouted. He was getting tired of her questioning. "Can't you see that? I had it, and then it was gone."

She didn't respond. Robert suddenly felt bad for yelling at her. All these years of missing her and wishing he could have her by his side, and now here she was, and he was shouting and angry. This wasn't the reunion he had imagined.

"I know this is hard, Robert," she pushed, "but I want you to develop greater sight so your vision can be restored. This won't work if you're going to cling so desperately to the perspective that limited your ability to see important things in your life.

"Life isn't some embodied being that walks around snatching things from people. Life happens, but it doesn't take things."

"Fine," Robert could feel his irritation and impatience rising again. "Things weren't taken, but they certainly left me," he spat out with bitterness rising like bile in his throat.

Robert couldn't see the wistful, understanding look that fell on his mother's face. She just stared at him for a moment, radiating empathy and compassion. He heard her stand and walk around to face him. She grabbed his hand, and he resisted the urge to pull it away. His childhood was filled with moments of this woman holding his hand and trying to provide comfort and care. He took a deep breath and tried to relax, to allow her presence to be the comfort he knew he needed.

"It's hard to have someone or something you love leave you, isn't it?" she said.

"Yes," Robert whispered. "I guess you understand that pretty well too." A faint touch of bitterness lingered in the statement.

"I do," she agreed. "And that's why I also understand the danger of the perspective that things are *taken* or *leave* our lives. It's a self-centered, myopic focus that prevents us from seeing the bigger picture. When we only look at the loss—the things that happen to us—we fail to see the opportunities, and how the events in our lives happen *for* us."

"Mom, how can you say that? Dad literally left us, left you! How was that an opportunity? That messed up our lives. It made everything harder, for you, for me, and certainly for Sandra."

"And sadly, Robert," she smiled, pressing his hand to her chest. "I let that pain sink deeply into my heart. And that pain lived there the rest of my life and exacerbated the pain of my breast cancer. Who knows, maybe it even caused it."

"Are you saying that Dad leaving us caused your breast cancer?"

"No," she answered firmly. "I'm saying that the pain I chose to carry, the things I chose to tell myself, may have. But the cause is not the important part, Robert. The important thing to understand is that I held it there. I let the pain tell me how to interpret my worth. And, whether or not it caused my cancer, it was a cancer on its own."

Robert wasn't quite sure how to respond. He felt the pain and resentment of his father's betrayal thrumming in his head. Memories swirled in his mind, stoking the emotions further.

"When hard things happened in your life, Robert, your focus went inward. You only paid attention to how they affected you and missed the effect it was having on others."

"That's not true, Mom, and you know it," Robert argued. "I saw how much Dad's leaving hurt you. I was keenly aware of the impact it had on Sandra too. That was a major part of my life before college."

"Robert," her voice was filled with compassion, "your focus was on how our pain was impacting *you*. And even though, in your kindness, you served us both through that time, your focus was still on what was happening to you—what you were losing. And so, your service didn't serve you. You didn't *see* what was happening."

Again, Robert was speechless. It stung, but he could see it was true. He fought back defensiveness. She wasn't attacking him. Reflecting on those memories, he could only remember his resentment. His anger. The assumed duty and loss of opportunity that had come into his life.

"Did you ever notice how happily Sandra lives her life?" his mother asked. "Her smiles and positivity? Hard things happened to her too, Robert. And yet she has chosen to be happy. Did you ever wonder why?"

"I don't know that I wondered why. I certainly wondered *how*." Robert reflected on how annoying her smiles and positivity were sometimes. It always seemed so naive and shortsighted.

"Did you ever wonder why she named Bobby after you?"

Chapter 19

The Incident

February 1961

I'm cold," Sandra complained as she pulled her yellow cardigan tighter across her chest. It didn't fully reach across her bosom, a fact that, before having to walk home from school in a gusty drizzle, she had been rather proud of.

"Well, maybe you should have worn more clothes," Robert rolled his eyes. "Seriously, Sandra, Dad would freak out if he knew what you were wearing at school."

"But he doesn't," she retorted with a shiver. "And it's going to stay that way because I'm sure he would be disappointed to find out that his only son was drag racing the family car last weekend."

Robert's head popped up, squinting through the pelting rain. "How did you..."

"Robert, everyone at school was talking about how you beat Jimmy Johnson in a Ford Country Squire."

A smile crept across his face. "Jimmy can't race worth beans."

"And his bad racing bought me some insurance so I don't have to be the only Sophomore prude in the school."

"You little fink," Robert spat as the two rounded the corner onto their street.

"I won't be one if you won't," Sandra smirked, knowing she had won.

"Yeah, well, it isn't just Mom and Dad knowing how you dress, Sandra," Robert feigned a responsible air. "I think you're attracting the wrong kind of attention."

"Don't be such a square! I've seen the way you look at Nancy Robinson in her short skirt and tight sweaters. It doesn't seem to bother you when she does it." Sandra quickened her pace as they approached their cookie-cutter house, wanting to be done with the conversation.

"Just sayin'," he called out to her as she ran up the empty driveway. Sandra had blossomed in the last six months, and Robert found himself clenching his jaw as he noticed even older men taking second glances at her. He hadn't heard her name in the locker room yet, but he knew what the guys at school were thinking, and it set him on edge.

The house was pleasantly warm as Robert kicked off his soaked, crimson Chuck Taylors next to Sandra's dull black flats. Sandra had evidently hurried off to her room to change and the front room was oddly quiet. Typically, their mother was there to greet them with a snack and a litany of questions about their day. Now, the knotty pine wood paneling, usually radiating warmth and comfort to the family room, echoed back the lonely silence. Robert roamed through the kitchen, looking for some sort of note from their mother to explain her unexpected absence. Finding none, he walked down the patterned turquoise carpet hallway to the bedrooms, passing years of family photos hanging on the walls.

"Mom?" Robert called out. "Are you home?"

No answer. The only sound was the shuffling noises of Sandra changing her clothes behind her closed door. Robert gently knocked on his parents' door before cautiously pushing it open. The room was a mess. Hangers were strewn across the floor, lying like dead bodies over abandoned and lifeless articles of clothing. Robert rushed through the door in a panic. His mom sat in the corner, head down, hugging her knees tightly against her chest. She looked up briefly to reveal red, puffy eyes and smokey mascara bleeding down her cheeks.

"What happened?" Robert asked, wide-eyed as he carefully stepped around the debris. Scanning the room, he noticed that one side of the closet was completely bare, except for a couple of empty hangers dangling from the bar. Half of the dresser drawers were slightly ajar, revealing empty space within. "Mom, what happened? Where's Dad?"

At the question, her shoulder began to shake, and she buried her face deeper into her knees, trying to escape Robert's bewildered stare. Robert stood there, eyes darting back and forth over the disarray, trying to piece everything together. At last, he crouched down and started picking up the hangers from the floor, not knowing what to say, embarrassed by his mother's emotion.

"What's going on? Why is Mom's room such a..." Sandra's voice drifted off as Robert replaced several hangers in the closet. She rushed over to their mother and embraced her. Tears of fear and confusion spilled from Sandra's eyes leaving dark, wet splashes on her mother's mustard yellow cigarette pants. She wrapped her arms around Sandra, trying to give comfort she didn't feel.

"We need to talk," their mother began, wiping her nose with her sleeve. Robert and Sandra stared at their mother in anticipation. "Your dad has left."

"When is he coming home?" Sandra asked naively.

Her eyes fell and tears started afresh. "Oh, sweetheart," she choked out. "I don't think he will."

"Why not?" Sandra questioned as fear rose in her throat. "Where did he go?"

"I don't know, dear," she cried, embracing Sandra again.

Robert stood silently feigning a stoic stance. Thoughts and worries swirled violently in his mind like a whirlwind, ripping his hopes and dreams of the future apart. "Did he say anything at all?

"He said he couldn't do it again," their mother said through her tears.

"Do what again?" Robert pressed. This wasn't making any sense to him.

"I don't know. He was reading the paper this morning and suddenly slammed it down on the table. When I asked him what was wrong, he just said he couldn't do it again."

"Mom, was Dad cheating on you?" Robert questioned. He could feel anger boiling up in him as he contemplated the implications of losing his father.

"No!" She exclaimed adamantly. "Your father would never do that. He's a good man."

"What kind of good man leaves his wife and family?" Robert demanded. Sandra cried, afraid of what was happening and the tension that was building.

"Robert, I don't know. He had one of those far-off looks he gets sometimes. He didn't talk much after that. It was like he couldn't even see me or hear me," she explained as she pulled Sandra in tightly to comfort her.

"He took the car too, didn't he?" Robert asked, ignoring his mother's explanation. He paced back and forth, kicking clothes and hangers out of his path. "I'll probably have to get a job."

Sandra and her mother's cries shook him out of his angry ranting. He looked down at them, seeing their emotion in a different light. His anger gave way to remorse and the wave of fear and sadness he had been trying desperately to hold back.

"I'm sorry," Robert spilled out, dropping to his knees. "I'm so sorry." He wrapped his arms around them both, joining them in the tearful chasm of loss.

Chapter 20

The Afterlife

W hen I died," Robert's mother started as she walked him down a path flanked by knee-high grasses, "I was looking forward to escaping the pain of my cancer. But when I crossed, my pain was just as acute. The only sign that I died was my father sitting at my side, smiling down at me."

"Your pain didn't go away?" Robert stopped walking, surprised. "Do you still have any?"

"Oh, no. No, I have long since replaced my pain with love and joy. But it wasn't an easy process."

"Well, at least you got to *see* Grandpa."

"Yes, that was nice," she said, ignoring the implied negativity. "But he didn't make it easy on me. He quickly pulled me up and hugged me. I don't think I've ever had a hug hurt so much. It was like knives pressing into my chest. He was just as surprised that I pushed him away as I was to still have the pain."

Robert slowed his walk. "Mom, why are we walking around when you know I can't see? I keep thinking I'm going to trip into something and it's hard to focus on what you're saying."

"Then just trust me. I *can* see."

Robert shuffled forward, flustered at his mother's lack of understanding. Her arm was linked in his, much like it had been towards the end of her life when he walked her along the beach. He led and supported her with such care then. He had been strong for that fragile woman, eroded through cancer and chemotherapy. He needed that strength from her now, but he couldn't feel it. The worry of what *might* be in the way was too ever-present.

"Robert, do you think I would let you walk into something harmful?"

"No," he answered quickly, "I just feel like I'm the one leading and I can't see where we're going. It's stressful. I'm not following your line of questions either. You asked about Bobby's name but then changed the subject entirely. What does any of this have to do with his name. I don't see how this is going to help me get my sight back."

"Robert, understanding isn't always linear. Sometimes, we can't see enough of the big picture to know where the missing pieces are and how they link the parts of our past and present together. You're more capable than you realize, and you can see more than you think, if you would put your attention in the right places."

Robert stopped walking. She pulled at him in surprise.

"Stop. You've said that enough. It isn't helping."

They stood quietly on the path, Robert's emotions thick between them.

"I'm sorry, Robert. I'm trying to get you to focus on something other than your lack of vision. That will never help you get your sight back. Feel your other senses and trust the people around you who are helping. If you want to experience more than your blindness, stop magnifying it with such intense focus."

She started walking again and he instinctually followed at the tug of her arm. Gentle breezes brushed around them, rustling the grass as it tickled against his leg. Robert waited for her to say more, but she seemed content to just walk to the music of leaves dancing in the treetops.

After a couple of minutes, Robert interrupted the silence. "How did you get your pain to go away?"

"I didn't get it to go away," she explained. "I just learned to stop holding on to it so tightly."

"What do you mean?"

"Sometimes our greatest trials become our favorite pets, Robert."

"Mom, that wasn't any clearer. Can you just talk straight?"

She squeezed his arm warmly. "Robert, the pain I had in my chest didn't start with my breast cancer. I had held it there since your dad left us when you and Sandra were kids. When he walked out, ignoring my cries and pleas, dragging those suitcases behind him, I felt like he had torn something out of me that could only be returned if he came back. But when I saw you standing in the room, filled with anger and resentment, and Sandra filled with fear, I vowed to myself to use that pain as a motivator to provide everything I could for you two. Every time I started to feel sorry for myself, that pain would push me into action. I would smile in defiance, laugh in rebellion. And you know what, Robert? Before long, that pain became my friend. My constant companion.

"So, when the cancer came, the pain wasn't new. I knew what to do with it. It just drove me to try to be the mom that you and Sandra needed. But the pain from my cancer was harder. Harder because I knew that it was going to take me away from you, when before, my pain had always kept me closer to you."

"Then how did you let go of it?" Robert asked. His mind was spinning. He had always seen his mother as so resilient and brave—he'd been amazed at her ability to just move on and let go of things. Her smile had been the sunshine in his cloudy days. Her laughter had given him hope when despair threatened to drown him. And now she was telling him that she had been in pain the whole time.

"Well, it took quite a while for your grandpa to convince me that it wasn't serving me anymore. I felt so justified in my anger and hurt. I was so mad at your dad for abandoning us. Mad that you two didn't have a father at such important times in your lives. Mad at not having a spouse to support me through the challenges of parenting emotional teenagers. Mad at the judgmental looks I got for being a single mother.

"Grandpa helped me to see that the anger and pain I was holding onto was creating a barrier for me to feel and accept love. I argued with him because I knew how much I loved you and Sandra. But I realized I couldn't accept or even see the love that others were giving. I didn't feel worthy of it. How could I be? My own husband had left me."

"Mom, I had no idea," Robert marveled. He grabbed her arm in his hands. "You were always so positive and happy."

"Yes," she agreed. "On the outside. And that was for you."

"I don't think I could have made it through my life without you, Mom," Robert said, gripping her more tightly. "You were my lifeline when I couldn't keep my head above the water. You gave me some shred of hope when Mary cheated on me."

Robert could feel his mother smiling at him. She had done it so many times throughout his life that he could almost see her bright face looking up at him.

"And in life, I could never fully accept that love from you," his mother whispered. "But now, I can allow it to pour all over me so I can soak up every last drop."

"How did you do it?" Robert asked. "I mean, how did you change?"

"A few things, Robert. First, I had to change my perspective. I had to trust that there was more to everything than *my* view of the story. And then, I had to forgive myself."

"Forgive yourself for what?" Robert asked. "Mom, you were practically perfect."

She laughed softly. "And your perspective of me was one that I couldn't see for myself. But I think we all carry around a list of things that we think we have to keep beating ourselves up over, logical or not. The longer I let my list get, the harder it was to see the reality that surrounded me and the more pain I inflicted on myself. And those wounds, Robert, made it impossible for me to forgive myself. I had to learn that beating myself up was *not* a form of penance. It never led to forgiveness or peace. It just made things worse."

Robert exhaled loudly. His list was long, and he didn't like looking at it. He didn't want to think about what he did wrong. Things happened to *him*. Others wronged *him*.

"And so you just forgave yourself?"

"Well, no, not at first," she explained. "I had to see things differently. You know, step back and look at it differently. Like you when you were working on a painting. Sometimes, we just get so focused on a singular part of something that we get lost and fail to see how it interacts with everything else. We lose perspective.

"The pain I experienced in losing your dad was so intense that I just couldn't step back and see *him*."

"Who?"

"Your dad."

"Mom, you couldn't see him because he left us," Robert blurted out.

"Not with my eyes, Robert. With my understanding. I needed to hurt, and I needed someone to blame my hurt on." She paused letting the silence carry the weight of what she was saying. "I tried to blame him. Tried to put all my hurt on his betrayal, but it didn't last. I kept wondering what I had done to make him leave. So, I shared the blame and harbored the pain. I couldn't forgive him, and I couldn't forgive myself, because I was too focused on my pain to understand and see."

"See what?"

"His pain."

Chapter 21

The Artwork

May 1984

Robert tried to convince himself that he was happy to be alone. After all, he could focus better on the restoration work if he didn't have to keep explaining things to others. He could put his full attention and focus on mixing the restoration paint and matching the colors. Normally, solitude was welcomed as he hammered away at a project. But today, his loneliness kept nagging at him.

Sandra hadn't spoken to him for a couple of days. He hadn't reached out to her either, but he had the excuse of being busy with his deadline to complete *The Garden Path* before the Olympic Art Festival. The curator required at least a week before they opened the exhibit, which, given the drying time for the final varnish, only left him a week or two to complete the restoration.

The painting stared down at him from the easel. Intimidation had held Robert at bay for the last few days, and he procrastinated by busying himself with many other small, random projects. Yet it continued to stare him down, begging to be finished. At last, he worked up the courage to finish the painting.

Rummaging through his paint drawer, Robert pulled various tubes and lined them up along his table. He arranged them from warmest to coolest—Pompeii Red, Terra Rosa,

Orange Ochre, Lemon Ochre, Terra Verte, Sap Green, Sevres
Blue, Ultramarine Blue, Burnt Sienna—before applying
generous globs to his palette. Each lay there, shiny inchworms
of color, waiting to be blended with careful precision. This
project would be different than most, as typically a more
minimalistic approach to adding paint was the recommended
practice. However, this restoration required the brushstrokes to
be thick to match the style.

Tentatively at first, and then with more confidence,
Robert mixed and matched the colors needed to restore the
damaged painting. He scraped piles of color with his palette
knife, holding it up to the painting and squinting his eyes,
checking for the right match. The shadowed areas came easily,
but for some reason, he uncharacteristically struggled to match
the colors where the light shone through the trees. After several
minutes, he pulled out a 3x5 card with a small square hole cut
from the center. Holding this against the painting allowed him to
see the colors fresh, isolated from the surrounding hues. This
served its intended purpose and Robert quickly adjusted his
mixing and matched the colors quickly.

The decision to use hog bristle brushes had been an easy
one. Though he was used to using smooth, synthetic brushes,
Robert knew that recreating the style Mr. Adenet had originally
used would be impossible to accomplish unless he used a brush
more consistent with the Impressionist's work. This meant
ordering a set of Escoda hog bristle brushes from Spain. He
pulled out a short flat brush and took a deep, measured breath as
he looked back at the painting.

He began with quick, speckled strokes of deep
aquamarine as an underlayer. Blending into the edges of existing
paint was challenging and Robert didn't feel the same freedom
to be completely loose in an Impressionistic style. Carefully
approaching the edges, he practiced a layering of colors closer to
the top of the tear at the frame. It felt awkward to put down so
much paint and he fought the urge to get tighter with his strokes.
Bit by bit, the dappled strokes inched their way down the length
of the mended tear.

Robert stepped back from the canvas several times to inspect the seamlessness of his work. He found himself procrastinating the contrasting areas of light and shadow, unsure of his ability to do the painting the justice it deserved. At last, he dove in, reminding himself that if he messed it up, he could wipe away the paint and try again.

Careful to match the direction and thickness of each stroke, Robert tested a small area where the light shone through the trees. A slow dance with the painting began. Stroke, stroke, step back, and pause. Stroke, stroke, step back, and pause. The insecurity-infused strokes were halting, and Robert could feel frustration rising in his chest as his head began to feel hot.

A gentle knock at the door interrupted the awkward rhythm just as Robert was getting ready to throw down his brush in exasperation. Thankful to have something to pull him away, he opened the door, brush tucked behind his ear. A pleasant smile greeted him on the other side.

"Oh, it looks like you've started," Heather said, looking at the paint on the end of the brush. "Can I see?"

Robert stepped aside hesitantly, worried she would see his struggle. "Sure. I haven't done much yet. The style of texture is so different from what I'm used to. Blending each stroke into the existing paint is quite the challenge."

Heather approached the painting with the same air as if it were a finished piece hanging on the wall, hands behind her back and carefully leaning in. Robert tensed, now appreciating the previous solitude. He bit his lip to avoid blurting out any excuses.

"Wow, Robert. I'm really impressed," she commented, still looking closely at the painting. "Have you ever painted this style before?"

He laughed awkwardly at her praise. She looked up at him, smiling through her glasses. "Not really," he sputtered. "I had one assignment in art school to replicate a variety of styles, but that was a couple decades ago at least."

"Well I never would have guessed," she looked back at the painting again. "You have real talent."

"That's nice of you to say," Robert said in a tone suggesting he clearly disagreed with her sentiment.

"No really, Robert. I've heard that Impressionistic paintings are some of the most difficult to restore. And yet here you are, pulling it off smoothly on your first try."

"I don't think smoothly is the word I would use." He felt awkward again as she used his name. What had Sandra said her name was?

"You're too hard on yourself," she looked up at him, pushing her glasses up to the bridge of her nose. "Not everyone can see things like you do. The artist always sees the imperfection. What I see here is beauty returning to its original state. It's wonderful."

"That's very nice of you to say." Robert looked past her at the painting. His eyes rested on the flowers lining the path. *Bless you, Sandra!* "Heather, has the committee decided on the locations for the paintings yet?"

She smiled at him for a little longer than usual before she answered. "No. Not all of the paintings have arrived. They were also wondering if you were going to be able to complete this restoration before the exhibit starts. It's always challenging to make changes in the middle of a showing, so if you're not, they'll put it closer to the end where blank space isn't quite as noticeable."

"I'll have it done," Robert answered quickly. He felt the determination in him rise again.

"That's what I told them, but they wanted me to check to make sure. It looks like you've got things under control."

Chapter 22

The Incident

March 1961

The stack of job applications absorbed the sweat from his hands. This certainly wasn't how Robert had wanted to spend his Saturday, but his father had left him no choice. He didn't know how much the mortgage or other bills were, but the sight of his mother crying over piles of bills was enough to tell him that the family wasn't making ends meet. He hated seeing his mother that way.

There had been many adjustments. Riding their bikes to school each day hadn't been too bad, except when the wind kicked up, which seemed to be most days lately. But having their mother gone to work, cleaning other people's houses, had been a challenge. Making dinner wasn't too hard, but eating it at times, was a chore. Neither he nor Sandra had much skill in it, though Sandra was the better of the two. It just didn't taste like their mother's cooking, and there wasn't nearly as much of it.

"Is your manager here?" Robert asked a pimply teenager standing behind the window at the drive-in movie theater. He had already turned in several applications, many of which were boasting to pay a couple of cents higher than the new federal minimum wage of $1.15 an hour.

"I'm the manager," the boy replied with a self-assured smile on his face.

Robert's eyebrows raised in surprise. "Oh, well, here's my application," he said, sliding the paper through the opening at the bottom of the window. He started to turn but the boy stopped him.

"When would you be able to start?" he asked.

"As soon as possible," Robert replied, hope rising in his chest.

"Tonight?"

"Um," Robert considered his plans to go out with friends that night. Then the image of his mother hunched over papers at the dinner table flashed through his mind. "Yes."

"Good," the manager smiled, looking more than a little relieved. "We had two employees quit last night and we're understaffed for tonight. Be here in an hour and I'll train you on the basics."

The "basics" turned out to be cleaning bathrooms and clearing out the trash. It wasn't quite the glamorous idea he had of bussing concessions to cars and getting to watch the newest movies. The toilets in the men's bathroom never seemed to get flushed and he was greeted with many fecal surprises behind stall doors. Wielding a woefully inadequate plunger, Robert attacked the clogged toilet, gagging and heaving. Unfortunately, all his art classes in school had taught him to pay attention to detail. Now that effort was filling his senses with unwanted information. He bounced back and forth between resentment for his father and commitment to his mother. Staring down at the pungent slurry, he understood why others must have quit the job.

The manager, Jim, turned out to be the son of the owner of the theater. He was the same age as Robert but went to the rival high school. Robert didn't like him. He could tell that Jim was the kind of manager that would just give Robert all the behind-the-scenes work that no one else would want. But his family needed the money, so, on his first night of work, he gritted his teeth, put his head down, and did whatever was asked of him.

It was well after midnight when all the cars had left, and the trash had been cleared from the car lot. Jim switched out all the lights and walked Robert out the gate and locked it behind them.

"So, when do I get paid?" Robert asked.

Jim chuckled. "Eager, eh? You got a girl you're trying to date?"

"Yeah," Robert lied. "Something like that."

"Paychecks are every two weeks. The next one comes a week from Saturday. Make sure you clock in and out, or you won't get paid."

The front door squeaked as Robert quietly stepped into the house. Jaw clenched, he paused and listened. Nothing. A light was on in the living room, which seemed odd for this time of night. He softly closed the door behind him and took off his shoes. Step by step, he moved from the entryway to the family room.

His heart raced when he saw his mother sitting up on the couch. Head down, it was difficult to see if she was awake. Crouching, he looked at her face to see if her eyes were open or not. He dared a few steps closer before he heard the heavy breathing verging on a snore. The clock on the wall showed 12:48 am. Turning down the hallway, Robert tiptoed to his room.

"Robert?" his mother's groggy voice startled him.

He closed his eyes and took a deep breath before turning. "Hey, Mom."

"Robert, why are you home so late? Your curfew was almost an hour ago. I was worried sick." She stared at him through squinted, sleepy eyes.

"Sorry, Mom. I won't let it happen again," Robert answered, hoping to end the conversation. He turned and began walking toward his room.

"Robert," an uncharacteristically stern voice called out, "don't turn away from me. Come back here. This conversation is not over."

He stopped walking but didn't turn. Emotions were rising in his chest. This was unfair. He shouldn't get in trouble. He was just doing his part to help the family. She didn't understand.

"Robert," she said more forcefully, "turn yourself around and come back in this room. If your dad were here, he…"

"Yeah, well, he's not here, is he?" Robert attacked, turning to face his mother.

"Don't take that tone of voice with me, young man," she spit back, clearly awake. "You will talk to me respectfully. I've been working myself ragged for weeks now to make ends meet and this is how you talk to me?"

He wasn't mad at his mother. But all the emotion, the bitterness, and anger breached his ability to contain it. "You don't think I know that? You don't think I see the bags under your eyes and how you stress over a stack of bills?"

"Then why would you come home so late and not tell me where you are?" Tears started down her cheeks. "I'm doing everything I can to keep things as normal as possible for you two, and all I ask is that you just follow the rules. Is that so hard? I've been worried sick about you, and I don't need any more worry in my life right now."

"Well, maybe if Dad hadn't been such a coward, we wouldn't be in this position." He regretted it as soon as it came out of his mouth. He winced as his mother's crying intensified. He stepped closer and took a couple of breaths. "I'm late because I got a job at the drive-in."

She looked up at him in shock. "Why didn't you tell me?"

"Because they gave me the job on the spot, and you were working," Robert answered.

"You could have left a note for me, or told Sandra, or something so I didn't have to worry all night." Tears continued down her face, words interrupted by her sniffing as her nose had started to run as well.

"And Dad could have stayed and then I wouldn't have had to get a job to make up for his lack of responsibility."

It hit a nerve. She sank, defeated, and sobbed. She buried her face in her hands and wept. Robert stood there, feeling his own bitterness, and hating the sight of his mother hurt and weak. He didn't know how to respond to her. He wanted to sit and comfort her, but he was still so angry at his father for creating this situation.

"I'm sorry, Mom," Robert said, tentatively. "I just kept looking at my future and couldn't see how we were going to make it work. I mean, how am I ever going to afford to go to college when we can barely keep the house and put food on the table? Maybe I just won't go to Chicago in the fall. I can stay and help here."

His mother's head snapped up with a fierceness in her eyes that he hadn't seen before. "You are going to college, you hear me? We will make it work."

Chapter 23

The Afterlife

Your dad was a product of the war," Robert's mother explained.

"What do you mean?" Robert asked. "Dad didn't serve in the war, did he?"

"Pearl Harbor happened when he was just twenty-one years old, and it threw the nation into a frenzy. Young men everywhere were getting drafted or voluntarily enlisting. It put so much stress on everyone. There was a lot of social pressure to do your part."

Robert thought about the pressures he had felt himself with the Vietnam War. He understood the looks and the judgments for not serving.

"We hadn't met yet. Just after Christmas, he and his friends got together and decided to enlist rather than wait to be drafted. I guess you had more control of where you would go and how you would serve if you did that."

"But Dad didn't serve in the war. Right?" Robert asked.

"Your dad gave in to the pressure of his friends and enlisted with them, even though he didn't want to. And as soon as he did, he felt trapped."

"He never said anything about this," Robert said, surprised.

"Well, about a week or so after he enlisted with his friends, your dad and I met at a dance. He was so handsome, and I flirted mercilessly with him. I could see that he was nervous, but I thought he was just one of those shy guys that didn't talk much. I couldn't see that internally he was staring death in the face."

"Mom, are you telling me that Dad served in the war?"

"Yes. We wrote back and forth while he was in boot camp. He and his friends started in January. I guess the need was high for soldiers, so instead of being in boot camp for the typical twelve weeks, he was there for only eight. He hated it. He never really said that in any of his letters, but he would talk about how scared he was to have to go off and kill or be killed.

"I got to see him before he was sent overseas. He looked so strong and lean, but his eyes were a shadow. He acted very brave for me and promised to write, but I knew there was something wrong."

"How did I never know any of this?" Robert tried to picture his dad as a young soldier. His perspective was rocked by this revelation. He had always been such a quiet and reserved man unless provoked by some form of back-talk from Sandra or him. Those were the scary moments where he came unhinged and would yell and get in their faces, lecturing them about respect. But it was rare to see him be more than passive and amiable.

"He made me promise not to say anything about the war," she explained. "He hardly spoke about it when he returned, and never spoke about it after we were married. So, I just didn't think about it all that much.

"I'm not sure what horrors he saw or experienced out there, but he came back sooner than I expected."

"Why?" Robert asked, listening intently to his mother's words.

"I'm not sure on all the details because he didn't ever tell me the whole story, but he got hit by some shrapnel when a mortar exploded by his platoon. I think he saw some of his friends die and that changed him. The record states he was discharged honorably with a Purple Heart, but it never said anything of his psychological state."

"What do you mean, his psychological state? Did something happen?"

"Again, I don't know the whole story, even now. He said it doesn't matter anymore."

"You've talked to him here?" Robert interrupted.

"Many times, Robert," she explained. "Like I said, I had to understand his pain before I could let go of my own, because so much of my pain was rooted in his leaving me. When I understood more, I was able to forgive him and feel compassion and love for him."

Robert didn't know what to say. All his life he had held onto a deep resentment for how his dad had hurt his mother and the family, and now here she was telling him about her love for him. Her voice was so genuine and peaceful that he yearned to look into her eyes; to understand and know what she was feeling.

"Robert, heaven is a place of love," she paused and squeezed his hand. "And you can't fully experience heaven without having that love inside you."

"But Mom, he left us," Robert argued. "How can you talk about loving the man?"

"What he did hurt me, true. It tore at my heart, and I cried myself to sleep many nights." She squeezed his hand, and he felt her face come closer to his. "But it also made me stronger."

"You're going to credit him for your resilience?" Robert scoffed. "Mom, that's on you, not him."

"No, Robert," she said, squeezing his hand again. "It helps me to see that this happened *for* me, not *to* me. Sometimes we have to change the way we look at our past in order to move past it. Our perspectives are so limited in life and that prevents us from being able to see the love and light in our life. We lose compassion for ourselves and others. We don't experience a fullness of joy.

"So, my father, wanting me to let go of the pain that I was holding on to, led me to see different perspectives in my life. And shifting that perspective, Robert, seeing the bigger picture, allowed my pain to melt away into love and joy."

Robert felt overwhelmed. So many of his paradigms were being shattered. If it hadn't been his mom talking, he would have rejected everything that was being said. *And what good would that have done me?* he thought. *I'd just be wandering around heaven, blind and angry and resentful.*

"Mom, why did you marry Dad?"

Her voice softened and after a moment's pause continued. "Like I said, your dad and I wrote throughout his time at war. We got to know each other very well through those letters. I got to see past the shy exterior and see a very sensitive man. I loved his thoughts and ideas. He wanted peace and harmony for all people. He spoke about the racism and bigotry he saw in the other soldiers and how much he hated it. He lamented about the loss of life, not just of American soldiers, but of the people dying throughout the world because of the war. He called it the Great Tragedy."

"And yet he was OK just randomly leaving his family and ruining their lives? Robert argued. As much as he was trying to listen and have compassion, he couldn't get past how incongruous her words were.

"It wasn't as random as you might think," she whispered.

"What do you mean?" Robert asked. "One day everything seemed fine and normal, and the next day he packed up his bags and we never saw him again. It doesn't get much more random than that."

"I struggled with that for much of that year," she reflected. "I needed to make sense of the abandonment. I searched for clues everywhere. Was he having an affair? Did I do something to drive him away? I had to know because it ate at my self-confidence.

"But I found pieces to the puzzle in that search, I just didn't know how it fit into the whole picture, because I didn't understand his pain."

"What did you find?"

"I saved the newspaper he had been reading before he left. I scoured those pages for weeks for something to help me understand what he meant when he said he couldn't do it again."

"And?" Robert prompted his mother as she faded off in thought.

"There was an article about President Eisenhower severing diplomatic relations with Cuba," she explained. "I didn't think much of it at the time, but then I remembered him telling me about his concerns with Castro turning Cuba into a communist country and how it would likely spark another world war. Then I started to make the connection to where his thoughts must have gone. He must have had some traumatic response and fled. He wasn't rational."

"So just reading some newspaper article convinced him to leave his family instead of protecting them?" Robert was incensed that his mother was trying to use this as a legitimate excuse for his dad leaving the family. "Mom, that's ridiculous."

She sighed deeply, and Robert could hear the disappointment. "Robert, in life, before you went blind, you suffered from myopia. You could only clearly see the things right in front of you. Don't let yourself do the same thing in heaven."

"What's that supposed to mean?" Robert asked, offended at the implication.

"You condemn your father, and anyone else, to the tragedy of your own perspective." Her tone was sharp, yet gentle. "I never said it was right that he left us. But if you want to see again, you'll need to get outside of yourself and stop limiting your sight to your own experience."

They sat quietly for a moment. She kept surprising him with her boldness and directness. It stung and he wanted to shy away from it. However, he knew there was truth to her words. He felt embarrassed at the immaturity of his responses, despite how easy it was to rationalize his words and reactions. They were the victims, not his dad.

"Do you want your sight restored, or should I let you live eternity the way you preferred to live in mortality—blind and full of resentment? It's your choice, Robert. You are the only one who can make that change for yourself."

"I didn't prefer to live that way, Mom," Robert said softly. Her words hurt deeply, but he was losing the will to fight back. There was clearly something he was doing that was keeping him blind, and fighting back surely wasn't helping.

"It was, Robert. Even when good happened, when people loved and served you, you couldn't see it. You focused on your resentment. You couldn't even see how much Sandra and Tom did for you once you were blind. They gave and sacrificed so much for you, but instead of gratitude, you focused on how she convinced you to get the surgery, the accident, and your blindness."

Robert opened his mouth, but nothing came out. She was right. His words of gratitude to his sister had always been for the sake of politeness. He rarely felt the words, usually just angry that others were having to care for him.

"You lived so many years from a victim mindset, Robert. It was hard for me to watch, and I didn't know how to help you in life. I just tried to love and support you, but I was never able to help you see the good around you.

"And then, I passed away and you let that fuel your victim narrative even more. You didn't notice all the people that surrounded you and Sandra with love and support. You only saw that you had lost me."

"Mom, I was devastated," Robert explained. "I was only twenty-seven and had been divorced for barely a year. I still needed you."

"I know, Robert," she stroked his hand gently. "The thing that was the hardest for me my last few days was knowing that I was leaving you and Sandra. Yet I took comfort in knowing that you would still have each other. But what you missed is that Sandra needed me just as much as you did. She was only twenty-four and had a young child to care for. Yet, she still saw your need and was there for you. She still accepted the joy and goodness in her life."

"Mom, are you trying to make me feel guilty?" Robert asked.

"No, sweetheart. I'm just trying to help you see that there was another perspective. Another way to experience a tragedy. There was still an abundance of love, even in the moments of scarcity. To restore your sight, you'll need to get past your myopia and focus on the big picture. Can you do that with me?"

Robert let out a heavy breath. "I'll try."

The Accident

December 1996

Tom eyed his wife as he drove through the intersection. She was tense and gripping the door handle hard enough to make her knuckles white. He worried about her. She still refused to drive, even a month later, and he could tell that she was racked with guilt over Robert's blindness.

"You OK?" he asked, hoping she would at least talk about her fears.

"Yeah, I'm fine," she lied. "Why do you ask?"

"Just curious." Tom gave up digging. She always put on that sweet, brave smile he fell in love with. He could see through it now, but when they met, he just saw an indomitable spirit. And maybe that's still what it was, but he just better understood all the fears, insecurities, and conflicts that her charm blocked others from seeing.

"Ok, I guess that's not totally true."

Tom perked up. "Oh?" He tried to stay nonchalant. He didn't want to act too interested and stifle any potential vulnerability.

"I just hate that Robert is all alone in that little house of his," Sandra began. Tom exhaled. This again. He felt the same way, and he loved Robert like a brother, but he couldn't stop his growing worry about his wife. "I mean, he's going to get hurt or starve or…"

"That's why we're going over there now, Sandra," Tom interrupted.

"I know, but *what if?*" She emphasized the last two words and looked up at Tom with doe eyes. Goodness, she was beautiful. "I just can't get the picture of him—blood streaming down from his face—out of my mind. And then I see him stumbling through his house trying to find something to eat and taking a bite out of something covered in mold."

Tom reached across the console and put his hand on her leg, his left hand securely on the steering wheel. He didn't know what to do or say about Sandra's guilt. He had suggested she see a therapist, but she turned him down quickly. So, to help Sandra, Tom had carved out time from his work schedule each morning and afternoon to check on Robert. In so doing, they had forged a meaningful relationship, at least Tom thought so. It was hard to get a good read on what Robert was thinking.

"What does he talk to you about when you're there?" Sandra asked.

"Just like I tell you, Sandra," Tom started, trying to be patient. She asked this same question almost every day. "I read the major news stories to him, we discuss anything in there, I ask him if there's anything I can do for him, he usually says no, and that's about it."

"But does he ever say anything about me or the accident?"

"Sandra, dear, you've got to stop beating yourself up about this," he squeezed her leg for emphasis. "I mean, do you want me to tell you that he hates you and thinks his blindness is all your fault?"

"Well, it *is* my fault, Tom," Sandra choked up. "Does he say those things?"

"No!" Tom breathed out. He wasn't sure if he was going to be able to convince her of this, and he could feel the tension rising. "Sandra, the only time he ever brings you up is to ask how you're doing. He loves you. You're his sister. I don't think that's going to change. Sweetheart, you've got to get over your guilt about this. It wasn't your fault. Someone crashed into *you*. You didn't even get a ticket. The officers at the scene charged the other driver with the responsibility because it was so obvious. Their insurance has been paying for the hospital bills and our car. Accidents happen. This one just had some really unfortunate consequences."

Sandra put her head down and took a shuddering breath. She always got quiet when he brought up the accident. *These two,* he thought. *They bottle up so much. Someday they're going to explode.* They drove the rest of the way to Robert's home in silence.

"He's doing better than you think," Tom said as he rang the doorbell. They waited quietly for a while, huddling closer together to fend off a cold wind.

"Should we just go in?" Sandra asked. "You brought the key, right?"

"Just give it a sec," Tom answered as he fingered the key in his pocket. "He needs to practice the independence of answering his own door."

"Yes, I know, but..." They heard scraping behind the door.

"Sorry, just a minute," a muffled voice came from behind the door. "Blind man struggling."

Sandra raised her eyebrows at Tom and nodded her head toward the door. Tom rolled his eyes and slowly shook his head at her. "He's fine," he mouthed.

The door opened and Robert looked out past them. "Can I help you?"

"Hey, Robert, it's me and Tom," Sandra said warmly.

"Tom," Robert started with a hint of a smile on his face, "I told you to stop bringing your girlfriends over. Sandra's going to find out."

Tom smiled and rolled his eyes as he looked down at Sandra. She wasn't amused and smacked Robert in the gut as she walked past him through the door.

"This one's abusive," Robert said to Tom, though his head was turned in Sandra's direction. "You really should stick with Sandra. She's much nicer."

Tom stepped up to Robert and grabbed him by the elbow. "Let's go in and see if we can't talk some sense into that sister of yours. She's still convinced that your blindness is her fault." Tom had said it in a joking manner, but Robert steeled for just a moment, long enough to speak volumes.

"Good luck," a hint of a smile returned quickly. "She's always been pretty stubborn. And Tom," Robert said, pulling his elbow away, "I can manage walking down the hallway by myself."

"Of course you can," Tom answered, hanging his arms awkwardly at his side.

They walked in, Tom following behind Robert. He noticed the darkened line on the wall as Robert reached his hands out and felt his way down the hallway. He made a mental note to get a cloth and clean the streak while Robert and Sandra talked.

"You need some Christmas decorations in here, Robert," Sandra said as she walked around the main room. "It's too drab for the holidays."

Tom gave her an incredulous look and drew his hand across his throat trying to get her to stop that line of thought. For as sensitive and thoughtful of a woman she was, sometimes she really missed the mark.

"Sandra," Robert said in a flat voice. "I'm blind. What do I need Christmas decorations for?"

Sandra cringed. "Oh, I'm so sorry, Robert. That was really thoughtless of me. I just want to brighten things up so you can feel the holiday cheer."

Tom watched as Robert shuffled through the kitchen, hands reaching for familiar counters and chairs until he reached the table. He assumed the position he always did when Tom visited, back to the wall, eyes staring unfocused up at the ceiling, listening carefully to the sounds around him. Sandra looked pained and she sat down next to her brother, placing her hand on his. She looked up pleadingly at Tom.

"It's fine," Tom mouthed to her. He didn't feel the same push as his wife to make everything all better. Robert was going to mope. He had every right to do so. His world had been turned upside-down and it would take a while to adapt. All this Tom accepted, and recognized his role was just to be there. Sandra just wasn't there yet, and no matter how many times Tom tried to explain that to her, she wasn't going to get it until she let go of her guilt.

"I know!" Sandra sat up straight, voice full of sudden cheer. "You have a CD player, right?"

"Yes," Robert's voice was a drab contrast to Sandra's enthusiasm.

"We need Christmas music!" Tom smiled at his wife's look of triumph. He loved how committed she was to help her brother, and everyone for that matter, feel the holiday cheer. Sandra jumped up from the table and Tom watched Robert for any change in his demeanor as she did her thing. Robert just closed his eyes and dropped his head, shaking it back and forth.

While Sandra rummaged through Robert's CD collection, Tom sat down next to him and whispered, "She won't stop until she sees you smiling."

"I know," Robert responded. "She can't handle people who aren't as happy as her."

"Well, this one is a little different," Tom explained. "She feels personally responsible for that discrepancy."

Robert's jaw clenched just enough for Tom to notice. He'd have to back off that topic for a while. He was a bit surprised at this because Robert had always taken the caretaker role with his younger sister. Now, there was a subtle coldness he hoped Sandra wouldn't notice.

"The Chargers lost to the Steelers 16-3," Tom changed the subject. "It was pretty pathetic. It's like they're determined to have a losing season."

Robert scoffed. "What about the Raiders and the 49ers?"

"Don't you listen to the radio? The Raiders play tomorrow against the Chiefs, so that should be interesting. But the 49ers lost to the Panthers at home."

"I thought you told me they were good this year." Robert was engaging in the conversation, but Tom could tell his heart wasn't in it like it used to be. He was going along to be polite now.

"They are, but this Panther team is surprising. I wouldn't be surprised if they made it to the Super Bowl."

"Robert," Sandra called out. "Don't you have *any* Christmas music?"

"Shameful, isn't it?" Robert said to Tom. Then, turning in the direction of his sister, "Not everyone likes Christmas music as much as you, Sandra."

"That's silly. It's just not the holidays without Karen Carpenter's voice serenading in the season. Tom, do we have any discs in our car?"

"I don't think so, but you can check," he handed her the keys and watched her walk out the front door. He turned to Robert who was looking vaguely at the ceiling again. "How are you doing today?"

"Meh," Robert continued staring off at nothing. "I've never really liked the holidays."

"I know this about you," Tom said. "But outside of that, how are you feeling?" Robert had been back in his house for a few weeks now, and Tom was still trying to get a read on how his brother-in-law was managing.

"Other than the obvious?" Robert answered sarcastically.

Tom looked intently at Robert's emotionless face trying to decide how hard to push. "No, including the obvious." He decided to push a little more.

"Tom," Robert turned in his general direction, "have you ever been blind before?"

This again. Robert always seemed to block any real expression of thought and emotion. It was starting to get annoying, but he understood. "No, Robert, I can't say that I have."

"Well, have you ever lost something that was incredibly valuable to you? Something you used and relied on every day?"

Tom considered answering that his car had recently been totaled but then thought better of it. He also thought about the time that Sandra had broken up with him while they were dating. That had been a surprise that hadn't made any sense at all. But obviously, she had come back, so it didn't count.

"Nothing like what you're going through," Tom decided it would be best to just let Robert express his experience instead of trying to relate to it.

"It's just something I don't think others can understand. I have constant reminders about all the things I'm missing. Christmas decorations, football games, people's faces smiling back at me. And the worst part is my job. Disability pay, as nice as it is, will never make up for the meaning and purpose that I felt restoring artwork. Nothing, especially some government service, will ever be able to compensate for that."

"Hmm," Tom considered. "That sucks pretty bad. Sounds like you're in a pretty dark place." Tom regretted his choice of words the second they came out of his mouth. But fortunately, Robert just laughed.

"You got that right," Robert smiled sardonically at the unintended pun. "How's work going for you?" Robert asked, clearly changing the topic.

"Oh, it's been alright. Sometimes working in HR can be a bit of a drain. At least we've been doing a lot more hiring than firing lately. It seems the tech industry is the place to be right—"

"Well, look who just showed up!" Sandra burst through the door in a flurry of energy and excitement. Behind her, Bobby strolled in, an awkward grin on his face.

Seeing the boy made Tom proud. He knew his son was busy with a new job in the tech industry, as well as with a girl he was dating, hopefully more seriously than some of the previous ones. Yet here he was. Unbidden by anyone, visiting his uncle.

"Sorry, Robert," Bobby said with a smooth, deep voice. "I didn't realize you had company."

"Oh, you don't have to apologize!" Sandra jumped in. "It's just great to see you."

Tom winced again. He looked at Robert for a reaction, but he maintained a stony face. Though, that seemed odd given the relationship he had with Bobby. Usually, Robert would brighten up and start spouting off ridiculous dad jokes whenever Bobby was around. He looked at Sandra with big eyes and raised eyebrows trying to get her attention. She looked at him, confused, and mouthed, "What?"

He realized she had no idea how what she said might be insensitive towards Robert, who *couldn't* see Bobby, but probably wished he could. She was just so genuine and happy all the time that her filter for the right thing to say didn't always kick in.

"I see you've resigned yourself to hanging out with old people," Bobby joked as he sat down next to his uncle. This got a smile out of Robert. So Robert wasn't completely closed off to good feelings.

"Well, you take whatever you can get when you're as pitiful as me," Robert joked back.

"Oh, stop that, Robert," Sandra smacked her brother on the shoulder. "You're not pitiful."

"Pitiful enough to be a punching bag," Robert looked in the direction of Bobby and gave a little smirk. Sandra just rolled her eyes. Tom was always amused at the sibling dynamic that would come up so quickly between these two. It was like a time warp. He would watch his wife change into a teenager right before his eyes.

"Do you want me to come back when these old fogies aren't here bothering you?" Bobby asked. "It might be hard for them to appreciate the literary genius of Douglas Adams."

Tom noticed Bobby was holding a book in his hand under the table. He couldn't read the title, but it was something about hitchhikers. Had Bobby been visiting more frequently? From their banter, this seemed to be more of a regular visit for Bobby.

"Just stay," Robert reached out for the handsome young man. "You might learn some respect from your elders. How's that new girlfriend of yours? Is she still as pretty as you described?"

Bobby looked up sheepishly at his mother before answering. "Yep, still as beautiful as ever."

Robert waited for more but was met instead with an awkward silence. "Is something wrong? Usually, you can't stop talking about the girl. Did you do something stupid and mess it up?"

"No, I just wouldn't want to bore you with my uninteresting love life," Tom could see that his son was squirming. He could also tell that it was in large part due to his mother looking in on the conversation like a vulture—circling and hoping for scraps of information.

"That's not what you thought last time you were here," Robert pushed. Again, the awkward silence. "Am I missing a social cue here? What's the blind guy missing?" He paused and looked unseeing around the room. "Oh, I get it. Your mother is here. Gotcha. I should probably shut up now."

"No," Sandra chimed in, "by all means, keep asking. The boy doesn't seem to want to say a word to his poor old mother who is just itching for some grandchildren."

"Aaaand," Bobby drew out the word, "that's why. Seriously Mom, why do you have to make it so weird?"

"Well, you're not getting any younger Bobby," Sandra chided. "Twenty-six is getting up there. Don't you think it's about time to settle down and have a family of your own?"

"Mom," Bobby rolled his eyes, "You talk like I'm some miser avoiding life and responsibilities. Do you want me to just marry anyone and then live a miserable life when she turns out to be crazy?"

"No, but you don't need to be so picky, either."

"What book do you have there, Bobby?" Tom interrupted. He knew from experience that this conversation would just lead to them both being frustrated, and for some reason, Sandra couldn't back down from it. Did she think that the pressure was going to help the situation?

"Oh, it's just the new Douglas Adams book," Bobby said, lifting it in the air, happy to be done with the line of questioning. "*The Hitchhiker's Guide to the Galaxy*. It's pretty funny, in a really dry way."

There was a bookmark poking out of the book about two-thirds of the way through it. Tom smiled as he realized that his son was coming to read to his uncle regularly. It warmed his heart to know that he was living the principles of kindness and thoughtfulness that they had tried to instill in him throughout his youth.

Tom sat back and watched his family, pleased that they were all working to turn a tragedy into an opportunity for love. What a contrast to the family dynamic he had escaped as a child.

What he would have done at a young age to be able to live the life he was living now. His wife was smiling and happy to be with her brother and son. His brother-in-law, despite his commitment to being grumpy and focused on his misfortune, was actually someone he enjoyed serving and spending time with.

This was the ideal, despite what life tried to throw at it.

Chapter 25

The Incident

April 1961

His bookbag was almost as heavy as the thought of how much studying he would have to do to pass the upcoming exams. Robert slung the bag over his shoulder and funneled slowly out of his physics class. Mr. Stimpson coughed as he erased the blackboard filled with equations and diagrams, chalk marks dirtying the back of his charcoal grey suit coat.

The hallway was a cacophony of chaos as students darted back and forth, slamming lockers and talking with friends. Robert tried to tune it all out as he stared down at the black and white checkered floor. Only a month more of this madness and he would be able to move on to the adventure of college. If he could save enough money.

A deep, artificial laugh rang out, making Robert's skin crawl. Joe Meecham. One of the most popular seniors in their class and a certified creep. At least, that's how Robert saw him. The girls in the school all seemed to fawn over him for some stupid reason. Maybe it was the perfect Elvis-like pompadour hair, stiff with who knows how much gel, that made them swoon. Or perhaps it was the fact that he was a starter on the school's football team. Robert thought it had something to do with the Pinehurst Green '59 Cadillac Coupe DeVille that his parents let him drive to school. Either way, Robert saw him for what he was: a phony. The way he would talk about girls in the locker room always got Robert's blood boiling. He couldn't understand why all the other guys thought he was so cool.

Taking a quick look to see what girl the victim of his greasy advances was, Robert's heart sank. Sandra. Her eyes had that dreamy glaze that girls of lesser intelligence would get when Joe graced them with his attention. She hugged her books to her chest, thankfully, as Robert noticed Joe looking her up and down.

"Sandra," Robert called out, trying to pull her attention from the slimeball. "Meet me at the benches today." They always met at the benches before walking home, but it was the only thing he could think of to interrupt them. Sandra gave him a weird look before turning her attention back to Joe. It was worth a try. He was going to have to pay closer attention to Sandra from now on.

Robert couldn't focus during his final class of the day. The teacher droned on about the world politics leading up to World War II. Yet all Robert could imagine was Joe trying to seduce his sister. *She's three years younger than you, Joe!* Robert thought. *Why are you giving her so much attention?* It certainly wasn't for anything benevolent. Irritation bubbled to the surface as he wished his dad were still with them to lay down a stiff boundary for Sandra to follow. Mom certainly wouldn't do anything. She was always too zoned out and tired whenever she was home. And she wasn't home often. Robert felt his resentment towards his dad grow even more. *What a selfish man!* Robert fumed. *Walk out on us for no reason, just we need you the most. Jerk! Now I have to be brother and father to Sandra because you couldn't handle life.*

Sandra was late to the benches. Robert paced back and forth, fluctuating between anger and worry. Why was she taking so long? Fists clenching and unclenching, he imagined Joe cornering her in some hallway and taking advantage of her. He was just about to walk back into the school to find her when she burst through the doors giggling with a flock of young girls in too short dresses.

"What took you so long?" Robert demanded.

"Jeez, Robert," Sandra frowned. "Cut me some slack. Do I need to ask your permission to socialize with my friends at the end of the day? You don't need to wait for me anyway. I'm old enough to walk home by myself." She walked past him to the crosswalk without pausing for him to follow.

"Hey," Robert hustled to catch up with her, "I'm just trying to watch out for my little sister. There are some real creeps out there, you know?"

Sandra walked faster, giving him a glare over her shoulder. "Ever since Dad left you've been a real bore. Stop it. You aren't my dad."

Robert clenched his teeth. Of course she would bring *him* up at a time like this. She needed a dad right now and she was blinded to the danger she was in. Dad leaving had forced him into this role, whether he liked it or not.

"Yeah, well, I clearly don't want to be him. If I were, I would have left you already." It was low, and Robert recognized it as hurtful as soon as it came out of his mouth. But he couldn't back down. She needed to understand the risk she was taking by giving any attention to Joe Meecham.

Sandra walked faster, clutching her books in front of her more tightly. Robert easily kept up with her smaller stride. Step for step they walked in silence for several minutes, Sandra refusing to look at him. Robert battled in his head, deciding what to say to her.

"I saw you talking to Joe today," Robert blurted out awkwardly.

"And you made it super awkward too," Sandra quipped looking ahead.

"He's a creep, Sandra. You shouldn't talk to him."

She stopped and turned toward him. "For the first time in my life, a good-looking boy gives me some attention and you're going to tell me that I shouldn't talk to him? That's real rich, Robert. Maybe you're just jealous that I have a social life." She marched off again in a huff.

Robert stood, jaw slack, not knowing how to respond. He decided to avoid the argument about his non-existent social life and stick to the most important issue. "I'm telling you, Sandra. The guy is a creep. You don't know him like I do."

"If you know him so well, why don't you avoid him then?"

"I do," Robert retorted. "Every chance I get. He's a real slimy person. He's not the kind of guy you want giving you any attention."

"Don't be such a prude, Robert," Sandra shouted. "So what if I've grown up a little and boys give me more attention? Is it so hard to believe that some boys might actually find me attractive? Did you even think that might be something I want?"

"I don't care if boys are attracted to you, Sandra," Robert lied. "I just don't want *that* boy to be attracted to you. He's bad news."

Sandra didn't respond. She just continued her quick march home, Robert lingering several steps behind. Robert fumed quietly, not knowing what to say and not believing she would listen to him either. They kept up their silence until they walked through the door of their home.

"Mom," Sandra called out. "Can you tell Robert to leave me alone at school? He's trying to ruin my life."

"Don't listen to her," Robert retorted. "I'm trying to help her, but she doesn't want to hear it."

Their mother was laying on the couch with one arm draped over her eyes. Her cleaning lady dress was well worn and could have used some cleaning itself. A pot sat on the stove steaming, filling the air with the smell of spaghetti sauce.

"Mom, all that happened was that an older boy was talking to me in the hallway at school and Robert just freaked out. It was so embarrassing," Sandra whined.

"The boy is a creep, Mom. You really wouldn't want that kind of boy talking to her," Robert said. They both loomed over their mother, who continued to lay motionless on the couch.

"Mom," Sandra prodded at her, "can you tell Robert to stop interfering with my social life?"

"Kids," she groaned. "I'm really tired. Could you go argue somewhere else?"

"But Mom," Sandra complained.

"No buts, Sandra," she peered up from under her arm. "I have to go to my other job in," she peered up at the clock, "about thirty minutes. I'm tired and I need a nap before then. Your dinner is cooking on the stove. Why don't you go see if the noodles are done cooking?"

"Why are you making dinner right now? It's only about three."

"Because I have to be at work at dinner time, so I got it started for you now," she answered, eyes still closed. "So why don't you be helpful and check on the noodles."

"Fine," Sandra said and stomped over to the kitchen.

"The guy's a real creep, Mom," Robert said softly, kneeling by her. "Sandra needs to stay far away from him."

His mother turned herself toward Robert, reaching for his hand. She looked exhausted and Robert could see dark circles under her eyes. He put his hand in hers and she squeezed it tightly.

"Robert," she began, "I know you care about your sister, and I'm thankful for that. Just consider her feelings, OK?"

"But," Robert interrupted.

"No buts, Robert. I'm really tired. I've been working hard since early this morning, and I still have another shift tonight. I don't have the time or the energy to deal with a petty argument right now."

"It's not petty, Mom. This is serious."

"Robert, I need some rest before I go back to work. Manage this like the mature senior you are."

"I am," Robert argued. "I'm telling you so you can stop her from doing something stupid." Robert stood and started walking toward his room. "If Dad were here…"

"That's not fair, Robert," Mom called after him. Robert kept walking.

Chapter 26

The Artwork

May 1984

Normally I don't have such a hard time with this," Robert said to Heather as he mixed paints and held them up to the canvas.

"It looks like you're doing a great job to me," Heather smiled.

"No, this style is so different from what I'm used to," Robert explained. "And there's a mood and emotion to it that is tickling at my consciousness, but I just can't seem to grasp. I think that's why I'm having a hard time matching the different layers of paint. For some reason, in my mind, it's more than just a color. Each layer has a distinct emotion. I'm afraid that if I don't match the emotion, the repairs will be fairly noticeable."

"Well, what you've done so far looks pretty seamless to me, and observing artwork is what I do for a living." She kept smiling at him. It seemed like she was paying more attention to Robert than the painting itself. She lingered longer than usual, and something about that was distracting. Robert wasn't quite sure what to make of her attention, so he tried to focus even more intently on the painting.

"You see here," Robert pointed with the back of his brush at a spot on the painting, "where the artist has brought the light shining in through the trees? If you look closely, between some of the brush strokes you can see the shadows peeking through. It's important to his style, and I've got to make sure I get those undertones right before I do the light."

"I think you figured out the shadows already," Heather observed.

"What do you mean?"

"Well, the parts you have already restored are in the shadows," Heather said, pointing to the spots on the canvas he had already completed. "My guess is that the theme of those colors," she pointed at another area in shadow, "carry on the same way even where there is light. The light is just covering up the shadows." She looked up at him with an innocent smile, like she had explained some advanced algebraic equation as if it were simple addition. "I mean, life is different. Light chases away the shadows if you let it in."

Robert just stared at her. She was right. It was that simple. In his efforts to make sure it was perfect, he had over-complicated the process. He looked back at the painting and saw through his defenses. He was avoiding seeing the solution because he was afraid of painting the sunlight and getting it wrong.

"Hmm, I think you're right. Thank you, Heather," Robert said, consciously using her name.

"My pleasure," she said. She patted his leg and stood up. "I'm always around. But I'd probably better leave you to your work and stop distracting you."

Robert didn't watch her leave. He stared at the painting, focused on the shadows. The dark and the light were there together. The light was placed on top. He could see it now.

Chapter 27

The Afterlife

Mortal life is a mix of joy and pain," Robert's mother started. "That's true for every person who has ever lived. The very nature of being mortal means that we will experience pain. Some pain can be traumatic, and other pain is essential to growth and change. Some pain is physical, and other pain is emotional or psychological. But our perspective of each is what matters most.

"A mother has to endure a lot of pain and discomfort to bring life into the world. And for most, the pain can be forgotten so quickly by the joy of holding the little child in her arms. I remember that experience well with both you and Sandra. I remember thinking that I would drown in the excruciating pain. I thought I wouldn't make it and that I would be one of those mothers who died in childbirth. But then, they handed you to me, and I couldn't even remember my pain through the joy of holding you.

"Life is like that, Robert," she held his hand in both of hers. "If you focus your attention on your pain, that's all you'll experience, and it will overwhelm your ability to see or feel anything else."

Robert listened. He reflected on all the challenges his mother had been through in her life. He had taken for granted her pains because she spent so much time smiling and encouraging others. His mind drifted to his sister, Sandra. She had endured many of the same things he had, and yet she always seemed to be almost annoyingly happy. However, his memories of his own life were flooded with bitterness, sadness, and malcontent.

"So how do I change?" Robert asked honestly.

"Change your perspective," she said. "Be willing to see the things that you failed to focus on in life so you can have a fuller view."

"Again, if I didn't see it in life, how can I see it now?" He wasn't trying to be difficult. It just didn't make any logical sense to him.

"Robert, your life had an undertone of challenges. A hue of sadness if you will. But overlaying that was experiences of goodness and hope. You just stayed focused on the pain and difficulty and everything that didn't go as expected," she stroked his hand in encouragement. "Let's explore all the bright colors that lightened your life despite the challenges."

"Will you help me?" Robert asked, a hint of pleading in his voice.

"Of course, Robert," he could hear her smile, remembering how much hope it had given him in dark times. "I'm going to ask you several questions and I want you to answer quickly, so your mind doesn't have time to add all the negatives."

"OK."

"What was your favorite thing in life while you were blind?"

Robert inhaled deeply. A favorite thing? How could he think of something he liked about being blind? It was awful. It was just darkness. It was…

"You're thinking too much," she prompted. "Just tell me something you liked during those years. Anything at all. It doesn't have to be big."

His mind flashed to sitting in his home waiting for Bobby to arrive. He always looked forward to his visits. "Bobby," he let out with a breath.

"What about Bobby?"

"He was always a bright spot in my day. He visited me almost every day. Sometimes for a few minutes, sometimes for several hours. But he always came." Robert reflected on this and realized he had felt happy when the boy was around. He could almost forget about his blindness during those visits.

"And what made those visits so bright for you?"

"He would read to me," he said, reflecting on the many books they had experienced together. "A variety of books. Humor, classics, fantasy, mystery...In the end, it didn't really matter what it was. It allowed me to transport myself to another time or place and forget about my blindness as I imagined the words of the story in my mind. And then we would talk about them."

"That boy was sweet from the day he was born. I wish I could have had more time with him."

"Oh, Mom," Robert turned to her. "You would have loved him. Even in his awkward teenage years, he was a joy. He always showed genuine interest in my work and asked such good questions."

She squeezed his hand. "I do love him, Robert. I never stopped watching him grow. I just didn't get to hold and talk with him like you did.

"Here's another question: What would your life have been like, after the accident, without Bobby?"

This was a question he had never considered. Had he just taken for granted Bobby's regular visits? He tried to imagine his life without him. As he did, the image of a sinking ship in a dark, tumultuous sea, taking on water, filled his mind. Bobby had been his life preserver. He had come at his darkest hour.

He remembered sitting in his house, seriously contemplating suicide. He hadn't seen a reason to continue living. His job was gone, his sight was gone, and now he was just a burden on others. While thinking about ways he could do it, a knock had come at the door followed by a shout, "Robert, it's me, Bobby."

"I think my life would have been much shorter," Robert admitted. "I probably would have committed suicide if he hadn't been there. He gave me a reason to keep going every day, and I never really acknowledged that fact."

"Good," his mom encouraged. "Keep going with that. *See* your time with him through that perspective now."

Robert closed his eyes, instinctively, to imagine his life anew. Memories flooded his mind. He could hear Bobby's subtle laughter interrupting his reading of Hitchhiker's Guide to the Galaxy. He smiled as he thought about how enthusiastic he had been to describe what the girl he was dating looked like. He could feel the joy and excitement he shared as he talked about his proposal to her. Meeting her had been such a pleasure because of how nervous he could tell Bobby was. He had fumbled all over, making things awkward. Robert smiled as he imagined the two mouthing words to each other and trying to act normal.

His heart swelled as he remembered the enjoyment of their company. The bitterness of not being able to see it all tried to creep in. It was like a blackness eating up positivity. But now, he saw the darkness for what it was—a refusal to accept his misfortune and move on. He pushed it aside and focused again on the good. His life hadn't been miserable—he had just chosen to focus on the misery of it.

"What are you noticing now?" his mother asked.

"My bitterness was my choice," Robert confessed. "I was stuck in my way of thinking."

"Good. And how did that affect your sight?"

"I didn't pay attention to the good that was there. I took it for granted."

"You see, Robert, even while the undertone of misfortune and disappointment was present in your life, goodness and joy were splashed over it like sunlight reaching down in bright rays through breaks in the clouds." She squeezed his hand again to emphasize her words.

"Now," she continued, "let's bring it back to the present moment. Close your eyes."

"Waste of time," Robert interrupted. "I can't see anyway."

"Just do it, Robert," she said, ignoring his quip. He closed his eyes and she continued. "Take some slow breaths and focus your attention on all you can experience right now. Don't let your mind get pulled into the past or focus on regret or disappointment. Just the present moment."

Robert focused on his senses. He could smell the earthy smell of the ground beneath him. There was a sweet smell of something nearby, either flowers or his mother, he wasn't sure. A slight breeze rustled leaves overhead and he listened to their movement. The sound rolled in a pattern, much like waves rolling onto shore. He imagined the treetops swaying like dancers to a slow, joyful song.

Sunshine warmed his skin and he breathed in the sensation like a solar panel collecting energy. He could feel its warmth move around his body as the shadows from the dancing trees swayed in harmony with the wind. With a breath, Robert tipped his head up toward the sun and felt it shine on his face. Shadows swayed back and forth across his eyes and the orange light of the sun glowed on and off through his eyelids.

Orange glow. Through his eyelids. That was color.

Robert opened his eyes.

Chapter 28

The Accident

May 1997

Taste the rainbow," she giggled nervously. Bobby loved that intoxicating laugh. She poured a couple of Skittles into Robert's outstretched hand. "You know, we just thought, maybe if you can't see color, at least you could taste it."

"I think it's brilliant," Bobby said, noticing his uncle's typical dark expression. "It was Felicia's idea. We were watching this stupid new Mike Myers movie last weekend and eating a bag of Skittles together. And then she turns to me, in the middle of the movie, eyes looking all magical, and says, 'Taste the rainbow!'"

Bobby couldn't tell if Robert was buying it or not. His expression was mostly unchanged, except for his eyebrows, which had raised just slightly. Was that amusement? Or was he playing his, "I'm blind" card again? Who knew? Bobby had learned to stop caring about whether or not he was going to offend his uncle. He needed to get over his gloom somehow, and so Bobby was going to help move that along.

He had been nervous when he had brought Felicia, his new fiancée, to meet Robert for the first time. That had gone horribly. Bobby might as well have been blind himself, with everything he kept tripping over. Why did a blind man have so many things in his house to knock over and break anyways?

And yet, despite all the awkwardness of it, Robert had smiled. And that one thing made it all worth it. If his uncle could smile during that mess, this couldn't be any worse.

"It'll be like a game," Felicia continued. "We'll each eat a Skittle, and then have to guess what color we have. Whoever gets the most right, wins."

"Don't you two think I'm at a distinct disadvantage?" Robert questioned as he smelled the candy in his hands.

"No," Felicia jumped in. "We were thinking you had the advantage. We go around relying on our eyes all day long. But you get to focus on all your other senses more."

It was thin ice they were walking on. Bobby knew it and he was watching Robert's expressions like a hawk. Felicia didn't seem to notice Robert clench his jaw just a little. She was just so beautiful, innocently smiling at his uncle. She looked up at Bobby, catching him staring at her with a questioning look on her face.

"I mean, if you don't think you can handle the competition, we can do something else," Bobby teased, hoping to ease some tension.

"Alright you two cheaters," Robert grumbled in an old, cowboy voice, "if you need to boost your ego by beating a blind old man in a silly game, I'll let you."

"You're so thoughtful," Bobby said sarcastically. Felicia just clapped her hands with that dreamy smile of hers that could melt an iceberg.

"How am I supposed to know that you two are telling me the truth about what color I'm eating? It could be anything and I wouldn't know," Robert asked.

"I guess you'll just have to trust a couple of cheaters," Bobby retorted with a wry smile. Robert wouldn't be able to see it, but he would know the smile. They had joked like this for years before he went blind.

"Ok, Robert, you have two in your hand right now," Felicia explained.

"I'm blind, Felicia, not numb," Robert teased.

Felicia hesitated and cringed. She was a sensitive girl and wasn't quite as used to Robert's dry sense of humor. Bobby touched her shoulder in encouragement.

"That's no way to talk to a lady," Bobby chided.

"I'm sorry, proceed," Robert bowed his head in apology.

"Ok," Felicia continued more cautiously. "Now close your eyes and put one of them in your mouth."

Robert looked up in her direction and raised an eyebrow. "So I don't see which one I put in my mouth?"

"Obviously," Felicia said. "What, just because you're blind you don't think you have to stick to the rules of the game?"

Robert laughed out loud.

Chapter 29

The Incident

May 1961

Mothra was a dumb movie. Robert knew because he had watched it now at least six times. He didn't mind getting to see all the new movies, but most of them lost their magic after the third or fourth watching. And Mothra was particularly bad. He didn't understand why all the girls acted scared. It just wasn't scary. Maybe it was so they had an excuse to cuddle up to the boy in the car. Either way, Robert thought it was stupid.

Robert walked around the aisles of cars picking up trash that the drivers couldn't be bothered to take care of themselves. The odd screeches of the big, stupid moth and the incessant beating of drums sounding out of the car's radios put his teeth on edge as he carried trash to the big waste bins near concessions.

"Hey Robert," his manager, Jim, called through the concessions window. "People are complaining 'bout the bathrooms being dirty. Go clean 'em, alright?"

They were thirty minutes into the movie, no one was getting any concessions. Jim was just sitting there doing nothing, other than watching the movie. Why couldn't *he* do it? Robert dumped the trash and went over to the janitorial closet to get the mop and other cleaning supplies.

He took two steps into the men's room and knew why Jim hadn't cleaned them. The smell was horrific. Worse than the typical bathroom smell. Someone must have exploded in here. Robert approached the stalls with caution, extending the end of the mop to open each door. And behind door number two was a nightmare more terrifying than Mothra.

Only surface tension prevented the burnt ochre slurry from spilling out onto the tile below. Toilet paper floated precariously between small chunks of feces. Robert imagined the result of sticking a plunger down in that mess and groaned. This was going to end up on his shoes, he just knew it.

Fifteen minutes and countless dry-heaves later, Robert emerged from the bathroom like a soldier from war. He looked to the concessions stand just in time to see Jim toss popcorn into his smirking mouth. For the umpteenth time today, he questioned whether this job was worth it.

"Next time, you can clean the bathroom and I'll man the concessions," Robert said to Jim as he pushed the mop back into the janitorial closet. "That was disgusting!"

Jim just laughed. He was so smug. It must be nice to have your dad own the place so you can just boss others around. Robert sat down on a bench just outside concessions. There was less than an hour left in the movie and there wasn't much left to do until all the cars left and he could do the final cleanup. He let himself get drawn into the movie to get the horrors of the bathroom out of his mind.

"Hey," Jim shouted, pulling him out of a stupor, "no sittin' on the job. Go pick up trash or something."

"I already…"

"Then do it again. We're not paying you to just sit there," Jim said as he sat lazily and munched on popcorn.

Robert just glared at him and picked up a trash bag to do another round. He knew there wouldn't be any trash at this point, but he left just to get away from Jim and the temptation to punch him in the mouth.

He walked along the back row of cars, looking up each aisle for any debris. Even in the darkness, the colors of the cars were enough to bring a bit of a smile to his face. He thought of the parking lot as a large palette with globs of paint waiting to be mixed and spread on the canvas above. There was Cherry Red, Chinese White, Mars Black, Saffron Yellow, browns on the woody station wagons, and Pinehurst Green…on a '59 Cadillac Coupe DeVille. Robert groaned. Joe Meecham. He wondered what unlucky girl he had seduced to come to a drive-in movie with him. He was sure that slimeball hadn't come to watch the movie or eat popcorn.

An empty popcorn container lay just outside the driver's side window. Of course Joe Meecham would just throw his trash out on the ground. No consideration for anyone else. Reluctantly, Robert started a slow walk down the aisle to pick up the trash. He didn't want to be seen by Joe, as that would surely elicit some sort of teasing.

A scream came from what Robert figured was Joe's car. It seemed ill-timed, as there weren't any of those cheap jump scares playing on the screen. Was this unlucky girl just playing the part of the dumb girl that gets scared easily so the guy would hold her in his arms? He knew girls in his classes who would do that. Robert wondered what Joe might be doing to the poor girl. He tried to look through the windows as he approached to check his hypothesis.

It was hard to tell for sure, but the two were clearly not snuggling in the middle seat. The girl was on her seat, scooting towards the passenger window, Joe in pursuit.

He bent down to pick up the trash outside the car and snuck a peek through the window to make sure the girl was OK. His heart stopped. The girl looked directly at him, pleading in her eyes.

Sandra.

Chapter 30

The Afterlife

Colors were back. Colors were back! Sure, everything was blurry beyond all recognition, but colors were back. Robert looked around at the smudges and shadows of green and blue, and the shapes of yellow and orange. His heart swelled as he breathed it in. Tears welled up in his eyes as he scanned around looking for his mother. He couldn't make her out through all the blur.

"Mom," he called to her, "are you there?"

"I'm right here, Robert." Her voice was so close. He turned his head in that direction.

"I can't see you."

"What do you mean? Did something change?"

"Yes!" Robert choked out. "I can see!" He reached around for her and marveled that he could see the movement of his arm. And when she reached out and grabbed his hand, he saw her too. He saw his mother. Well, sort of. There was no detail whatsoever. It could have been anyone, really, but it was her, and he could see something.

"Oh, Robert!" she exclaimed. "That's wonderful. How much can you see?"

"Not much, really. But I *can* see color. It's not all dark anymore. It's loose approximations of shapes, but the *colors* are there, Mom."

She hugged him. He could see the brown of her hair as she came close. The grey was gone. At least, from what he could tell it was.

"Thank you," Robert whispered in her ear as he hugged her back. "How did you do it?"

"I didn't do anything, Robert," she pulled back, holding his shoulders softly in her hands. "You did this."

"But how?"

"What did you just see that you hadn't before?"

Robert stopped and reflected. With all the color and excitement he had forgotten what they had been discussing. Something about Bobby and Felicia…and his utter refusal to see any of the good in his life.

"I saw that I was a bitter old man intent on staying that way," Robert admitted.

"No, I think you saw something more than that," she prodded.

"Mom, that's really what I figured out. I was intent on only seeing my own misfortune," Robert insisted.

"And it's good that you had that realization. But that isn't enough to restore the sight you lost," she explained. "It may be diagnostic, but not restorative. Knowing the cause of the darkness is good, but you had to see the light as well in order to chase the dark away." She paused and held him there, blurred features staring him down. "What was the light you saw?"

Robert considered what he had been thinking for a moment. "I was loved and cared for despite my gloom," he said. "Bobby saved me and brought a light into my life that I failed to acknowledge. He made sacrifices to be with me, even while he was dating and after he was married. He brought laughter into my home. I didn't see it for what it was at the time." Robert's shoulders slumped. Why had he wasted so much of his life focused on his misfortune?

"He *was* a light for you," his mother agreed. "But Robert, remember, heaven isn't a place for regret and sadness. You can't change the past, but you *can* experience it with a fresh perspective and soak in all the love that was there. Don't turn back to what limited your sight in the first place."

"What do you mean?" Robert asked.

"You can't change your past," She started, "nor would that help at this point. You have to live in the moment and let love be in every moment. Experience the good of the past like it's your present and let it fill your heart. Leave your mistakes behind and do now what you couldn't do then."

Robert let the words sink in. Let love be in every moment. That had surely been a challenge for him in life. He had taught himself to be wary of love because of how deeply he had felt betrayed by Mary. In nearly every moment he was scanning for how someone or something might not be genuine in order to protect himself from the possibility of getting hurt. And so, he had lived his life reliving his hurt rather than experiencing the love that was all around him.

"How do I let go of the resentment and fear, Mom?" Robert asked.

"I remember having that same question as I struggled to let go of my pain with your father," she reflected. "I wanted a simple solution. Something that would just take it away."

"And what was it?" Robert pressed.

"There's no magic solution, Robert. It takes effort and risk," she explained.

"Risk?"

"Yes. It comes down to trust." She paused to give the words emphasis. "It's a vulnerable feeling to trust. You have to put yourself out there, not knowing the outcome. Love given is never a mistake, and love received is a gift to both. You decide what you want to focus on. Fear is just a choice of focus."

Again, Robert had to think about what she was saying. What *had* been his focus in life? He thought about his father and his absence. Mary and her betrayal. The accident and his blindness. Then it clicked. His mother had been trying to tell him all along. He was focused on what he lost, rather than what he still had. Even when things entered his life to fill the void, he wouldn't let it in. Love lost overshadowed love given.

"Robert, you were a good person, despite the things you lost," his mom touched his face. He leaned into the warmth of her hand and smiled at the color he could see. "You gave love at important moments, whether you realized it or not."

"This bitter, old curmudgeon?" Robert joked.

"Yes. Despite your bitterness, you still loved. You meant the world to Sandra. You filled a hole in her heart after Dad left. Sure, you guys bickered and argued unnecessarily, but you watched out for her like a father would. She talked to me often about how much you meant to her."

"Really?" Robert said, surprised. "Why didn't she say something to me?"

"Oh, she did. Often. But I think you missed it because you were so focused on how your dad should have been the one to do the things you were doing."

"Well, that's true. He should have been there," Robert quipped.

"Robert, you're missing it again," his mother said firmly. "You were more to her than just an older brother. You were a lifesaver. I asked you earlier if you knew why she named Bobby after you. Have you figured it out yet?"

"No," Robert admitted.

"It's because of what you did for her. She always reflected on it with me."

"Mom, Sandra did more for me than I ever did for her."

"Robert, she did all that *because* of what you did for her. And she loved you deeply for it."

The Incident

May 1961

The rich smell of Aqua Velva made Sandra want to melt into the seat of the fancy Cadillac. She was swooning, and she knew it. But how could she not? She was going on a date with a senior. And not just any senior—Joe Meecham, star of the football team and every girl's dream. Sandra pinched herself. It wasn't a dream. Somehow, she, a simple sophomore, had caught the attention of this hunky specimen of a man. She enjoyed the look of envy she got from the other girls when he would stop and talk with her. She felt important. He made her feel beautiful as he complimented her hair and outfits. Sure, his eyes lingered a little too long in some areas, but that was true of most boys.

Joe was a perfect gentleman. He opened the car door for her, he complimented her, and he even bought the extra big bucket of popcorn for the movie. Robert had said that the movie was dumb, but he said every movie was dumb. Sandra didn't care. She was at the drive-in with Joe Meecham!

They talked about the end of the school year and how excited they were for the summer. Joe told her all about his summer plans and his chances to play football at the college he was going to. Sandra didn't really listen. She kept getting lost in his blue-green eyes. Eyes that kept drifting down past her neckline. Maybe she shouldn't have worn such a tight sweater.

She was surprised to feel a little relief when the movie started because Joe's eyes looked out the front of the car instead of at her chest. The popcorn sat between them on the seat. Sandra's heart went all aflutter each time their hands happened to touch each other. She let her hand linger a few times in hopes that he might reach over and hold it. Halfway into the movie, they found the bottom of the bucket and Joe finally grabbed her hand.

He smiled a big, charming smile down at her. "This is better than popcorn."

Sandra smiled back a bit bashfully and squeezed his hand in response. Joe lifted her hand out of the bucket and took the bucket with his other hand, tossing it out the window. With the barrier gone, he scooted a few inches closer to her and reached his arm around her shoulders.

It felt nice and she moved in the rest of the gap to tuck in tight to his side. She could feel his muscles flex under his thin, button-up shirt. How did she get so lucky?

Casually, but uncomfortably, Joe's hand relaxed from her shoulder and floated ominously below her collarbone. Sandra figured he was just relaxing his arm a bit, but she didn't like how close it put his hand to her breast. As she tried to shift her body to move away from the hand, her breast accidentally skimmed his fingers. Or had his hand moved?

"I'm sorry," Sandra said, embarrassed at the contact.

Tom smiled down at her. "Oh, I didn't mind." He reached down and briefly groped her. He maintained the smile as he looked into her eyes. Her skin crawled.

Was she supposed to like that? It was so shocking she didn't know what to do or say. She just looked back at him with an awkward grin on her face. Why couldn't she say something? Why couldn't she scream out or slap him for his impropriety? She looked back out at the screen, unable to focus on or hear the movie. How had she felt so relaxed just moments ago? Now her muscles were tense.

"How are you liking the movie?" Joe asked.

"Um, it's OK, I guess," Sandra replied flatly.

"Do you want to make it more interesting?" Joe asked, smiling at her.

Sandra's heart began to beat uncomfortably fast. "What do you mean?" Her voice quavered.

Joe put his hand on her knee, just below the hem of her dress. He kept smiling that awful smile and moved his fingers up her leg a couple of inches under the fabric. Thankfully he stopped, but that smile just glared down at her. Again, she froze. Her mouth wouldn't work. Joe's other hand reached down and grabbed her breast again. His strong arms pulled her body in tight so she couldn't move away. His hand slid up her leg a few more inches to her mid-thigh pulling her skirt up as well.

What was happening? How had this date suddenly gone so wrong? She was boiling with terror inside. How did Joe think this was what she wanted? She remembered Robert's vehement instance that Joe was a slimeball and groaned.

Somehow, Joe misinterpreted her sound of disgust and moved his hand the rest of the way up her leg. Finally, her discomfort breached her lips and she let out a scream. Shocking Joe, he relaxed his grip on her for a moment, long enough for Sandra to scoot away from him. She slid her back up to the car door and pressed against it trying to get as far away from this boy as possible. He just smiled bigger.

"Getting more comfortable?"

What? How could he even think that? She realized in her haste to get away from those awful hands that she had leaned back to be more prone. He turned and moved toward her, hand reaching for her waist. Panic froze her again as his fingers slid up and underneath the front of her sweater and moved up her ribcage. Desperately, Sandra looked out the window, hoping for anyone to walk by and see her distress.

And then, blessedly, a man approached and picked up the popcorn bucket from outside the car. As he bent down, they made eye contact. Robert. Blessed Robert. Here to save her from this awful situation. Her eyes screamed at him to do something. Just as Joe's fingers tugged down the front of her bra, trying to find the skin beneath, Robert knocked hard on the top of the car.

"Get your filthy hands off her!" Robert shouted with an uncommon firmness.

Joe's face went steely cold. Sandra watched in fear as his jaws clenched and he turned his head toward Robert. He pulled his hands out of her sweater just as Robert opened the car door and grabbed him by the back of his shirt.

Sandra had never seen Robert so intense as he pulled Joe back out of the car. Joe's shirt ripped and the top two buttons popped as he fell backward out of the seat and onto the ground. Robert kicked Joe hard.

"Never touch my sister again!" Robert shouted through clenched teeth punctuating each word with a kick to Joe's side.

Sandra watched in both horror and relief as her brother raged. She'd never seen this intensity from Robert. But he was much smaller than Joe. Joe came to himself and scrambled to his feet amidst the barrage of Robert's kicks. People were now taking notice and she watched as men, young and old started to get out of their cars.

Joe charged Robert. Like the football player he was, he slammed into him, shoulder first, wrapping his arms around him and slamming him hard into the next car over. It made an awful crunching noise and the girl in the car screamed. The men started shouting and running to intervene. A strong, dark-haired man from the car just in front of them got to Joe just as he punched Robert in the face. She couldn't see Robert through the surrounding crowd anymore and she curled up tighter in the seat. This was all her fault. Why hadn't she listened to Robert? Why had she let Joe touch her like that? Everything was going so horribly wrong.

Through the commotion, she could hear Robert shouting. "He was groping my sister! Didn't you hear her scream?" And then he burst through the crowd and was there crouching at the door. The side of his face was red and starting to swell.

"Are you OK?" Robert asked, concern written in his eyes.

She couldn't hold it in any longer. Tears erupted and she buried her face in her hands. But her hands couldn't contain the great racking sobs that shook her shoulders. "I'm sorry," she managed to get out. *What must he think of me?*

"Oh Sandra, this isn't your fault. He's a dirtbag. *He* did this to you." Joe was shouting profanities at Robert as men held him back. Robert reached his hand out to Sandra. "Come on, let's get out of here."

Sandra nodded and took his hand. She avoided Joe's angry stare as men pulled him away. She let herself be absorbed into Robert's gentle embrace as he walked her down the aisles of cars, drawing the attention of the people watching, wide-eyed, as they passed. Robert walked to the front gate, past the concessions stand where the manager came rushing out to stop him.

"What the hell do you think you're doing?" Jim shouted.

"I'm taking my sister home," Robert answered curtly.

"You hit a customer!"

"Who was attempting to rape my sister!" Robert shouted. Sandra could feel her face getting hot. She tucked her face into Robert's chest.

"You can't hit a customer, Robert," Jim sputtered, looking wildly at the crowd and commotion they had just walked away from.

"I can hit that one," Robert muttered through clenched teeth and kept walking Sandra toward his bike, locked up in front of the theater.

"Hey, you can't leave!" Jim shouted.

"I can, and I'm taking my sister home." Robert's voice was so strong. When had he become so protective?

"If you leave, you're fired!" Desperation was starting to show in the manager's voice.

"Then fire me," Robert said, not looking back. "And while you're at it, make sure you ban Joe Meecham from ever coming back here again."

The manager just stared at them in shock.

Chapter 32

The Afterlife

Robert tried to remember what he had ever done for Sandra that would have caused her to be so kind and serviceable to him throughout their lives. "Because of the Joe Meecham thing?" Robert asked, realization flooding in.

"Yes, Robert," Mom answered. "Your presence and protection at that moment meant the world to her. And before you go popping off that it should have been your father, just stop and think. How would he have known to be there?"

Robert stopped. He had spent his life thinking that his *father* should have been the one to save Sandra at that moment. *He* should have been the one to pull Joe off of her. *He* should have been the one to take Sandra home in his arms. But why would he have been at the drive-in that night? Would he have been there to spy on his daughter while she was on one of her first dates? No, Robert realized that wasn't realistic. Robert's presence at the drive-in had been fortunate. Walking down the aisles to pick up trash just when that was happening? Improbable.

Love and compassion began to fill his heart. He allowed himself to feel the situation from Sandra's perspective. She didn't resent that it wasn't Dad who had intervened. She was just grateful he had been there at the moment. That he had stepped in. That he had saved her from that awful experience. Robert allowed himself to feel her love and to let go of the resentment that had blocked him from doing so for so many years.

Tears of joy welled up in his eyes and he laughed. He laughed at himself for his short-sightedness. For missing the sweetness of love because he was so focused on a resentment that turned out to be more of an impossibility. He let gratitude rise to the forefront of his memory. He had been able to rescue his sister from being raped, and all it cost him was a lousy job and a punch in the face.

"You're right, Mom. I couldn't see what was right in front of me because I was so stuck in my self-inflicted darkness," Robert admitted. "I wish I hadn't wasted so much of my life missing out on what I'm feeling now."

"And what's that?" his mother asked. She leaned in toward him and sunshine illuminated the side of her face. He could see the distinctive rise of her cheeks as she smiled broadly at him.

"Gratitude and love," Robert wiped the tears from his eyes.

"Isn't it beautiful?" she asked. "Now think about Bobby again, from that new perspective."

The boy had always been a bright light in his life. He had been born only a couple of weeks after his divorce had been finalized, and the beauty of a new child had filled a bit of the hole in his heart. Robert Thomas Newsom, born on the twenty-eighth anniversary of the bombing of Pearl Harbor. His birth brought light into the world amidst the memory of a very dark day. Named for his uncle, who brought light to his mother at a very dark moment. How fitting that the boy would bring the pattern full circle by bringing light, many times, into Robert's darkest moments. Realizing this had been the key to bringing light back into his eyes. To see color, and to feel hope.

"What a gift he was," Robert said.

"And what a gift *you* were, Robert," his mother returned. "It's easy to disregard the good we do in our lives, but it's no less important."

"Thank you, Mom. Thank you for helping me to have the sight to be able to see."

"We aren't quite done," she cautioned. "Can you see perfectly yet?"

"No," Robert answered. "But I do think it keeps getting better. Things are getting a little more distinct. I can differentiate a broader spectrum of hues."

"Until your sight is completely restored, we aren't done."

"So, what am I missing?" Robert asked.

"You have to open the doors to healing and love," she explained.

"Isn't that what we've been doing?"

"Yes, and no," she said. "We've been exploring the things you failed to see in life. What I'm talking about now is the very thing that allowed my physical pain to go away here in heaven. Do you remember what I told you?"

Robert nodded slowly. "Forgiveness." Robert's stomach and jaw tightened. His father's abandonment wasn't something he thought he could let go of. It had shaped so much of how he saw the world during his adult life. He had come to expect that people would leave him. Even in his marriage with Mary, he had tried to fight back the feeling of impending loss and abandonment through their whole relationship. Every time he returned to their apartment after work, a part of him panicked, anticipating her being gone. It was the reason he kept people at a distance. And now, his mother was telling him he would need to forgive his father for that? Impossible.

"Robert, sometimes forgiveness isn't deserved," she started. "I questioned why your dad left us for years. I was sure that there must have been something I did wrong. And you know what I finally realized?"

"What?"

"It wasn't my fault," her voice was firm. "Which allowed it to be his fault, and actually, that hurt even more. I could explain away his actions with something that was in my control. But there wasn't something I could have done to change it. And that, Robert, left me with anger."

"Mom," Robert exclaimed, "I never saw you angry."

"Oh, I tucked it away so you kids couldn't see it. But it sat there, deep in my heart, inflicting a pain that lasted into the afterlife. And the only way to get rid of that pain was forgiveness."

Robert exhaled, feeling deflated. *I guess my sight will never be restored. There's no way I can forgive that man for what he did to us.*

"Forgiveness is a gift, Robert," his mother explained. "A gift to them, and a gift to yourself. Be generous."

"I don't know how to let go of this, Mom," Robert said. "His abandonment defined so much of my life, and not the good parts."

"Oh?" his mother asked. He could almost see her eyebrows raise in a questioning look. "Not the good parts? Are you sure about that?"

"Mom, how could Dad leaving us define anything good in me?" Robert asked.

"What things developed in you because Dad left?"

"Bitterness, resentment, hesitancy to trust relationships…"

"Can you see how you're approaching this the same way you approached the rest of your life?" She looked at him steadily. "Only focused on the negative. Unwilling to see the good that's there. What was the result of your unwillingness to see the good before, Robert?"

"OK, I get it," Robert blurted. "But Mom, that was different. That was me only focusing on what I lost so I couldn't even see, quite literally, the good that was around me."

"And help me to understand how this is different, Robert."

"Well…" he stopped. It hit him like a punch to the stomach. It was the same thing. Sure, it was different in minor ways. He wasn't blind because his father left, but he was fatherless. It altered the way he had to live his life. He needed to grow up faster and be more responsible. Getting a job to help pay for the family's bills as well as his college expenses prevented him from experiencing much of the typical senior year activities he had looked forward to.

"This isn't different, Robert," she said. "You focused on the loss and only looked for how it hurt you. You failed to see how it strengthened you."

"How it strengthened me?" Robert asked, incredulously.

"Think about it, Robert," she pushed. "What did you have to become when your dad left?"

"I had to do what he should have been doing," Robert said.

"No, Robert. Again, you're focusing on the negative. The loss. What did you *gain*?" She reached for his hand and held it in hers. "Your father leaving, as much as it hurt me, made me so much stronger. So much more capable."

"It made you more tired and unavailable, Mom," Robert retorted.

She paused and took a breath before continuing. "Robert, that's unfair. Yes, I wasn't around as much as I had been before. But do you know why?"

"So we could actually pay the mortgage," Robert answered quickly.

"That's only a part of it. I got one job to be able to pay for the house. But the second job? That was to pay for your college."

"That's why I got *my* job," Robert said. "I wanted to do what I could so that the family wouldn't suffer."

"And would you have developed that selflessness and consideration if your dad had stayed? Would you have been able to see outside of your own little world?" she asked.

Robert felt defensiveness start to boil up again. He didn't want to go there, though. He wanted to continue in the joy and light he had experienced just moments ago. So, with a deep sigh, he considered what his mother was saying. Would he have been the responsible team player he had been for those years? Probably not. Working at the drive-in had toughened him up and helped him to develop a work ethic, as much as he hated working there. He had also learned to see his mother differently. He had always taken her love and support for granted before his father's betrayal. But, with him gone, he was able to see her sacrifice. He had been mad at his father for making her have to sacrifice so much, but he could see it.

"No, I wouldn't have," Robert admitted grudgingly.

"Robert, the past, like our present, happens *for* us. It shapes and builds and guides us. When we learn to let go of our sense of victimhood, we're able to see and embrace the blessing of each moment, no matter how hard or challenging that moment might be."

"So, are you saying that Dad leaving us was a blessing?" Robert's tone was skeptical.

"No," she answered quickly. "But I am saying that it blessed our life in a very difficult and challenging way. Life isn't one-dimensional. Tragedy can be a blessing if we let it.

"For example, my cancer. As painful and unfortunate as it was, it brought my children closer to me. I got to spend my final days in the love and embrace of my children. I am so grateful for that."

Robert contemplated the implications of what she was saying. What if he had accepted his situation instead of marinating in the bitterness of it? How would things have been different? How would they be different now? As he imagined it, he began to see his bitterness as a tether, holding him down and keeping him away from the heights of a new perspective. Away from joy and love.

"Why do I hold on to bitterness and resentment so tightly?" Robert asked his mother as the realization hit him.

"If you're like me," she squeezed his hand, "it's because you don't want to let go of the way you were planning and expecting your life to be."

Robert nodded. That was true. So much of his life was spent angry at how others had altered the way his life should have been. A broken home, a failed marriage, a career cut short. None of it was his fault. He *was* a victim. But his life had been defined by this mentality and he had been miserable because of it.

He closed his eyes and imagined himself letting go of the bitterness of his father's actions and accepting his life for what it was as a result. He felt his heart being tugged in two directions.

One side felt the panic of letting go of the familiar; the reassurance that the pain was not his fault. The other side felt hope. Light. Freedom.

The Artwork

May 1984

Brushstrokes of pale orange and warm yellow moved almost effortlessly across the canvas now. Heather's observation had unlocked his perception and allowed him to step into his fear. This seemed to happen often when working on a restoration—getting stuck, not necessarily for a lack of skill or ability, but for fear of messing the painting up. It had been especially bad with this one, as the Impressionist style had forced him into a new way of seeing the project. There were layers of texture, and the layers were important. They provided a sense of depth and light that other artworks had not.

Light had been made tangible. A presence to overlay the shadow. Contrast accenting the very soul of the painting. He was starting to see it come together now, and excitement bubbled up within him. Robert even ventured a smile as he stepped back from the painting.

It was blending nicely. At this rate, he was sure he would be able to meet the deadline for the show. Just a few more spots to repair.

Chapter 34

The Accident

May 1997

S andra couldn't sleep. Tom lay next to her breathing in a slow, steady rhythm. How did he fall asleep so fast? It was probably because he didn't see shattering glass and blood every time he closed his eyes.

It had been nearly six months since the accident, but the flashbacks still haunted her. The ache in her neck had faded within the first few weeks. The scars on her hands had even started to fade. At least that was what Tom kept telling her. She wasn't sure if that was true or if he was just saying it to make her feel better. Either way, it didn't matter. Nothing he could say would take away the images that flashed through her mind at night. Try as he might, it also didn't change the feeling of panic every time she got in the car. And it certainly did nothing to make Robert see again.

She stared at the ceiling through the darkness. Even with the lights out, she could still see the ceiling. The faint red glow of the alarm clock pulsed next to her. Guilt returned as she thought about Robert. His blindness. The melancholy at having lost his career. The surgery she had encouraged him to get. The car she hadn't seen smashing into them. The legal and insurance settlements they were having to navigate.

For the next hour, she fitfully attempted to fall asleep. No position was comfortable enough to coax her past the thoughts and lull her into that peaceful oblivion. At last, a warm hand reached out and grabbed her by the waist.

"Hey, you need to go to sleep," Tom whispered in the dark.

"I'm trying," Sandra retorted. Did he really think she was trying to stay awake? She was exhausted. The thing she wanted most was sleep. It had just been so elusive lately.

No response. Did he fall back asleep already? She let out a defeated breath. Why couldn't she shake these thoughts? For the most part, she was good at moving on from hard things. Her mom's death had shaken her to the core, but it never affected her sleep. So why now?

"Is it the accident again?" Tom scooted toward her, wrapping his arm around her body and cradling her into his. He was so warm, and his embrace eased some of her tension.

"That's part of it," she answered. "I see the glass and my hands all sliced up. But then I see Robert and the blood dripping down his face past the sunglasses that the LASIK people gave him, and my mind just spirals from there."

"It wasn't your fault, babe," Tom reassured her.

"But it kinda is." Why couldn't he see this point? "I'm the one who suggested the surgery. I'm the one that was driving the car. If it weren't for me, Robert wouldn't be blind."

"You suggested the surgery because you loved your brother and wanted him to be able to see better. But you didn't force him. You just gave him information. He chose to get the surgery."

"If you suggested some surgery to me and I somehow died in the process, would you feel guilty?" Sandra had thought this argument through hundreds of times.

"I would be heartbroken to lose you, Sandra," Tom answered. "But I would never have suggested a surgery for you that wasn't for your wellbeing."

"What about a boob job?" Sandra interjected.

Tom laughed. "Babe, I would never suggest that. You can't improve on perfection."

His sweetness annoyed her. "I'm serious, Tom. I just feel so guilty." She could feel the tears coming and she didn't want to go there tonight.

Tom held her closer. "It's not your fault," he whispered in her ear. "None of it. Not even the accident. You had the right-of-way. You were driving carefully like you always do. The other car crashed into *you*. He ran the red light. We've been over this a hundred times. You've got to get over it, babe. All this guilt isn't good for you."

"So how come Robert blames me for his blindness?" That was the deeper issue. She was doing everything she could to help him. To make up for this awful thing that happened to him. To try to make it better in some way. But he just stayed cold whenever the topic came up.

"He's never said it was your fault, Sandra," Tom said. But she knew he had seen it too. The clenching of the jaw, the coldness, it was clear.

"He doesn't have to say it. I can feel it," Sandra whispered. "If only he could just acknowledge that it wasn't my fault, then maybe...But I just feel guilty."

"I can't say it enough times, babe," Tom propped himself up on one elbow and looked at her. "It. Was. Not. Your. Fault."

Sandra turned her body toward Tom. "Then why do I feel so much guilt?"

"I keep asking the same thing," Tom answered. She looked up at him staring at her through the darkness. "I'm starting to wonder how much of this has nothing to do with the accident or the blindness. It feels like old pain."

"What's that supposed to mean?" Sandra asked. Sometimes this man could be so cryptic. "Is that supposed to be an age joke? Maybe you're hanging out with Robert too much."

"No, Sandra, I'm not joking. Don't be so sensitive," Tom said, a little annoyed. That bothered her. If he didn't want her to misinterpret, then maybe he should be more clear. "I'm talking about old issues that you feel in the present."

"That still doesn't help, Tom," Sandra said, starting to feel annoyed herself. "Just tell me what you're trying to say."

"For the longest time, you talked about your gratitude to Robert for saving you at the drive-in when you were a girl. I mean, wasn't that the whole reason we took him into our house after his divorce?"

He was right. Dang it, he was right. She had gone back to that feeling of needing to repay Robert for that moment thirty-some-odd years ago. Maybe it wasn't just that she felt the need to repay him. It truly was love and gratitude for him as a brother. She hated the darkness and gloom that always seemed to permeate his mood. Why couldn't he see how good he was? Why couldn't he see how much people loved him? That was really what she wanted. For Robert to see that despite the awful things that had happened in his life, the abandonments and betrayals, he was still loved. And then, he went blind. On her watch. Because of something she had suggested.

"Yes," Sandra answered finally. "I guess it is old pain. I thought I had moved past it when Bobby was born. I guess not."

"Look, Sandra, I love Robert too. He's a good guy underneath that grumpy attitude. But that's the thing; he's a grumpy guy. That's just a part of him. You could give him the world and he would focus on all the pollution. You could give him a masterpiece painting and he would find the blemishes and cracks. That's just the way he is. You aren't going to change that," Tom reached over and touched her chin. "You're a good sister. You've out-paid him for any service he may have done for you. And that's who you are. You just love people and serve them as much as you can. That's one of the reasons I married you. You are amazing. Don't let his inability to see the good around him darken your spark too."

Sandra laid quietly in his arms for a while. She had come to a similar conclusion when she held Bobby in her arms all those years ago and peered into those sweet, innocent eyes. He radiated light and happiness and joy. She had honored Robert's selfless act in naming her firstborn son after him. Robert had been delighted by it. But it didn't change him. Sure, he was happy and kind whenever he was around the boy, but he was still Robert.

"Yeah, you're right," Sandra whispered through the darkness. "Thanks for reminding me. It just breaks my heart that he's blind."

"Me too," Tom agreed.

Sandra knocked on Robert's door. She wished he would just give them a copy of the key again, so he didn't have to crash through his house to answer. And what if he got hurt or disoriented and couldn't get to the door but needed their help?

The door opened.

"Wow, that was quick, Robert," Sandra said. He stared out the door past them. She hated that sightless stare. His eyes had started to go a milky color and she wished that he would just close his eyes like other blind people.

"Well, I don't have a very big house, Sandra. The front door is only about twelve steps from my living room sofa," Robert said. He looked left and right, not quite making any eye contact. "Is Tom here too?"

"Sure am," Tom said. "You lucked out again."

"I thought I could smell something," Robert said, straight-faced.

Sandra hated that she couldn't tell if he was being serious or not. He always had that dry sense of humor and she thought he used it purposely to be able to say the things he was thinking and then write it off as a joke.

"The smell of heaven is quite distinct, I must admit," Tom joked. "But that's Sandra, not me, Robert. Easy to mistake, though, so I forgive you."

Robert chuckled with a single breath and turned back into his home. Sandra and Tom followed, assuming the invitation.

"I love what you've done with the place," Tom commented.

Sandra smacked him in the arm. Seriously, the man could be so insensitive sometimes. Everything was disheveled and slightly askew. Of course it was. He was blind. Couldn't Tom understand that saying something only brought attention to his blindness? Sandra absentmindedly began straightening everything.

"You don't have to do that," Robert said as he sat down on his couch.

"Do what?" Sandra asked, pulling her hands behind her back.

"Fix everything," Robert answered. "I can't see it, so it doesn't matter what it looks like."

How did he know what she had been doing? She'd been so quiet about it. Maybe some of his sight had come back? Her heart fluttered for just a moment. "What makes you think I was fixing things?" Sandra asked with false innocence.

"Because you always do. You've been doing it for years, Sandra. Why would you stop now?" Robert looked vaguely in her direction. "I'm guessing you're just doing it quieter now."

"Well," Sandra said as she straightened a few more things, "I was just impressed with how clean everything is."

"And I'm sure it will be perfect if you stay long enough," Robert joked. It bothered Sandra though. Couldn't he see she was just trying to help? Well, no, he couldn't. He was blind. But she realized he had a hard time seeing that she was trying to help when she suggested he get LASIK too. She chuckled to herself. He had a hard time seeing then, too. She realized that Robert had always had a hard time seeing.

"What's so funny?" Robert asked.

"Nothing," Sandra lied. "I just had an amusing realization. Sorry."

Robert raised one of his eyebrows as he looked in her direction. She cringed a bit and scrambled to think of something to say to change the subject.

"So how have you been, Robert?" Tom asked. *Bless that man*, Sandra thought.

"For the most part, fine," Robert answered. "I'm starting to get the hang of things around here. I've pretty much got the house memorized now. I don't venture out much, so not much stumbling."

"Well, that's good," Tom said. "What do you do to occupy your time?"

"I listen to the radio, or old albums," Robert answered. "I'm glad I have a remote to the stereo. I also sleep a lot, which doesn't require me to see at all, so that's nice."

"I've noticed that about sleep too," Tom answered sarcastically.

"What can we do to help?" Sandra asked, rolling her eyes at the banter.

"I don't know, things are mostly OK," Robert answered.

"Well, we'll keep bringing you groceries," Sandra said, walking over to the refrigerator. "How are you doing on supplies?"

Tom gave her a funny look. "What?" she mouthed back at him.

"Sandra," Robert said, "you brought me groceries a couple days ago. I hardly eat, so supplies are pretty good."

"Well, you never know," Sandra said, opening the refrigerator anyways. "Boys eat a lot and I can't have my brother going hungry." It was awkward to say, and she knew it, but she just felt so awkward. She didn't know what to say that wouldn't attract more attention to the fact that he was blind. So she did what she knew how to do; serve.

Tom and Robert talked together about some hockey championship while Sandra looked through the refrigerator and took inventory. Robert was right; he didn't eat much. That worried her a little. She wondered if it was because there were just too many ingredients and not enough meals. She remembered how much more Bobby would eat when there were things he could just grab.

"Have you eaten lunch yet, Robert?" Sandra asked.

"What?" Robert asked. They clearly cared more about grown men skating around with sticks and hitting each other.

"Lunch. Have you eaten any yet?"

"No."

"Ok, I'm going to make some then." She began pulling things out of the fridge, planning on how to make enough that he could have easy leftovers for several days.

Twenty minutes later she had a piping hot pot of goulash ready to go. She called the men to the table and set the pot down on a hot pad at the center of the table.

"Smells good," Robert commented. "What is it?"

"Goulash," she said with a smile.

"You really are just like Mom," Robert said, feeling for his chair and sitting down.

"Thank you," Sandra replied.

They sat and ate, mostly in silence. It pained Sandra to watch Robert eat. He was so sloppy as he tried to scoop food onto his spoon, spilling noodles onto the table. He probably had no idea how much of a mess he was making. She realized that this probably wasn't the best meal for him. She kicked herself for not thinking of that before making such a big pot.

"Sandra, are you OK?" Tom asked. He must have noticed that she wasn't eating.

"I'm fine," she answered a little too quickly.

"Aren't you going to eat?" he asked. "It's really good. You outdid yourself."

"I'm eating," Sandra said. "I'm just not very hungry I guess."

Robert continued to struggle to scoop the food on his plate. Sandra winced as he consistently spilled food from his spoon.

"Do you want help with that, Robert?" she asked.

"I can feed myself," Robert answered.

"Are you sure? It really wouldn't be any problem." This wasn't working and Sandra could feel her anxiety build.

"Sandra," Robert started firmly, "I'm a grown man. I can feed myself."

"Yes, but you just keep missing…"

"I'm fine, Sandra." Robert's impatience was accentuated by another spoonful spilling onto the table.

"Robert," Sandra steeled herself for a moment. "I'm sorry about the accident, and I'm sorry you're blind. I feel terrible about it. I just want to help."

Robert didn't answer. He closed those sightless eyes and clenched his teeth. All three sat in tense silence. Tom looked at

Sandra, an eyebrow raised in a questioning glance. She shrugged her shoulders, a pained expression on her face. This is what happened every time she tried to bring it up. Every time she apologized. Silence. Punishing and condemning silence. Any response would be better. At least she could know where she stood with him. How could she move forward if he couldn't?

"Robert, I'm sorry. I wish none of this had happened," Sandra started up again. She looked up at Tom for support. He looked at her sadly and shook his head. He signed for her to stop.

"Me too," was Robert's reply. "Me too."

Chapter 35

The Afterlife

Robert basked in the blurred kaleidoscope of color. His heart was full of gratitude as he lay on his back looking into the sky. He had missed the array of color and light so much. While he couldn't distinguish between the hues and shades much, he didn't allow himself to complain. He didn't want to ruin this feeling. Heaven was becoming significantly more heavenly.

"There's a freedom that comes from unburdening yourself from your hurt and resentments," his mother said, breaking the silence.

It was true. He could remember all the emotions he had toward his dad. He could even still feel them. But he didn't have the same compulsion to dwell on them. To let them consume him. The weight of it all had been lifted. For the first time, Robert realized that it was his choice. His choice to wallow in the darkness of bitterness, or wade into the light of forgiveness, love, and gratitude. He was pretty sure he preferred the latter.

"Thank you for helping me to see that, Mom," Robert said.

"I'm not sure you fully do yet, Robert."

"What?" Robert sat up in surprise. "I do, Mom. I'm enjoying it right now. I'm soaking in color for the first time in decades."

"Robert," his mother explained, "you have smelled the aroma of a great feast. But you have yet to really partake. I'm glad you're enjoying seeing color again, but your sight has not been restored. There's still much that you're missing."

"What am I missing now?" Robert said, conscious of the urge to be defensive.

"Whose fault was the accident that ended up taking your sight?"

Good feelings faded into familiar darkness. Images swept through his mind, gripping at deep, unsettled emotions. The intensity of feeling surprised him even after all these years. He had never really been able to quiet the internal boiling. He had always just shut his mouth tight and tried to avoid hurting anyone's feelings.

"I'm not sure," he answered coldly.

"The tone of your voice would say otherwise," his mother said. She was always so good at reading through what he was thinking. Usually, that was helpful, but this was not one of those times. This was something he wanted to keep buried.

"And what does my tone say?" Robert asked flatly.

"What do you think it says?" she returned, warmth radiating in each word. "You asked me to help you, and it won't help if I do all the work."

Robert clenched his teeth. She was going to make him do this. Why did people always bring it back to this? The memories started to claw to the surface like a shadow reaching out at the sun's setting. He felt himself getting hotter as energy surged up within him. He struggled to keep his resentment at bay. His memories of his thoughts and experiences of the accident were shrouded in blackness. Bitterness sparked back to life within him.

"What are you thinking, Robert?" his mother nudged him softly.

Looking back in the direction his mom was sitting, his heart froze. The vibrancy of color was fading. Greens and yellows and oranges were becoming more muted.

"Mom, what's happening?" Robert asked, panicking.

"I don't know, Robert. What do you mean?"

"The colors are going away," Robert explained. "Everything is moving towards gray. What do I do?" This was a nightmare he hadn't even imagined. To have the colors come back and then fade away; it was more than he could bear. It was cruel.

"Well, what triggered the change?" she asked.

"You, asking me a question about the past," he answered a little too quickly. He noticed his tone and regretted it the moment he said it. Everything started to darken. "No, no, no," Robert panicked. "I'm sorry, Mom. Make it stop."

"I'm not doing anything, Robert," she said calmly. "You need to notice what's happening and why."

"It's hard not to notice. Everything is going dark again. I can't do this, Mom." Robert's voice cracked as his throat tightened and tears began to well up in his eyes.

"Are you noticing why it is happening?" she asked.

"No," Robert answered quickly.

"How did you lose your sight in life?"

"Retinal detachment after the car accident," Robert answered automatically.

"No, Robert. Again, that's how you lost your vision," she said softly. "How did you lose your *sight*?"

This stopped him. The difference between sight and vision. She had talked about it so many times. Was his vision in the afterlife more closely connected with his sight? How did he lose his sight? The darkening landscape distracted him with worry, so he closed his eyes to block it out. At least this darkness was by choice.

Robert strained to think about all the things they had discussed, but the dread of losing his vision a second time threatened his memory. It was like a cloud of gloom encompassed him, making it difficult to see past his present fear. He froze. That was it. A cloud of gloom. Or a cloud of anger and resentment. He tended to focus on the negative and to allow that emotion to paint everything he saw in the same hue, eliminating his ability to see all the other colors.

"It was my myopic focus on the negative things in my life," Robert admitted. "But I'm not quite sure how this fits here."

"Your focus on the negative is a part of it, Robert," his mom said. She placed a hand on his knee. "But your thoughts and beliefs about those events is another part. The interpretations that you hold onto define what you see all around you. So, keeping that in mind, I'll ask you the question again. Whose fault was the accident that led to you losing your vision?"

A single color flashed through Robert's mind. It wasn't one he saw, but one he remembered. Yellow. A single yellow circle of light shining through his memory. A color that he had chosen to push back and not talk about because of all its implications. And it came with accusations.

"Sandra's," Robert whispered.

"And why do you believe that?" she asked.

"Because the light was yellow when we went through the intersection before the car hit us."

"Hmm," his mother paused, thinking. "And what are your beliefs about that?"

"What do you mean?" Robert asked.

"I'm sure you attached some meaning to that event. Some belief about the way things should have been."

Robert hesitated. This had always been brewing right under the surface whenever he thought about his blindness. "If she would have stopped, this never would have happened."

"Alright, so you believe that if Sandra had stopped at the yellow light, you wouldn't have been in the accident and you never would have gone blind?"

"Yes."

"And did she ever apologize?" she asked.

"Often."

"Did you ever forgive her?"

Robert didn't answer. How could he forgive her? She had ended his sight. His career. His one joy in life. Letting go of that would be like giving her a free pass for her careless behavior. That was too hard.

"No," he finally admitted.

"And what has been the cost of that choice?" The question was so straightforward; it shook Robert.

"What do you mean, Mom?" Robert asked, not wanting to think about it.

"What has been the cost to your life and hers for not being willing to forgive her?" she asked plainly. "Think about it, Robert. This choice seems to have had a rather large impact."

Robert dropped his head as he considered the question. "Are you saying that my blindness is returning because of my resentment?"

"I'm asking you to consider if it is, and if that is the only cost."

Robert hesitantly allowed himself to consider. He knew the feeling of darkness. Blindness had only been a part of it. Darkness had always been about more than his eyes. It had come in a flood the moment his mother had asked the question. He felt it. It colored all of his emotions. All his sensations. It had been his companion most of his life. For some reason, he felt it as a protection. That surprised him. He considered the revelation. In his current state, it didn't make any logical sense, but he couldn't shake the sensation. What could the darkness have possibly protected him from?

"I'm going to need some help with this, Mom. There are too many confusing feelings," Robert said.

"Ok," she replied, "let me ask you a few more questions then." She paused for a moment and sat closer to him. "What emotional effect does your resentment to Sandra have on you?"

"I feel angry," Robert admitted.

"Do you like feeling angry?" she asked.

Robert wanted to say that no, he didn't. He knew that should be his answer. But as he considered it, that wasn't entirely true. A part of him did like feeling angry. He felt self-conscious with the realization. Admitting it to himself was hard, but admitting it to his mother was harder.

"No answer?" she probed.

"I don't like my answer," Robert said.

"Why not?"

"Because I know that I shouldn't like being angry," Robert answered.

"So, ask yourself what you like about being angry. How is it serving you?"

Robert pondered this. He appreciated the lack of judgment from his mother. He had anticipated more shock or even disgust when he admitted to liking the anger, but her curiosity settled him. He could look at the emotion with curiosity. He let himself feel his anger. It spread through his body like a drug, poisoning him with false power. His head burned, narrowing his focus. It felt like the blinders trainers put on a horse to keep them from getting spooked in a crowd. Then it hit him. The anger let him not have to focus on the big picture. It channeled his energy into one thing: Sandra.

"I think I like it because I don't have to think about anything else. I don't have to see the other things at play. It gives me focus," Robert explained. "It's like the blinders on a horse, preventing me from getting distracted."

"Distracted from what?" she asked.

"All the other things," Robert said.

"Yes, you said that before," she challenged, "but you didn't say what those things were."

He hadn't. It hadn't been intentional, but it wasn't an accident either. It was just easier to avoid looking at what his anger was covering. He opened his eyes to look at his mother and was met with darkness.

"It's gone," Robert said, thick with emotion.

"What's gone, Robert?"

"My vision," he whispered. "Everything is just darkness again."

She didn't respond immediately. Instead, he felt her come closer and wrap her arms around him, bathing him in warmth and understanding. "Robert," she started softly, "I find it interesting that you compared your anger to blinders on a horse. Blinders. And then you lament about being blind. That sounds to me like you want to be blind. That blindness protects you from having to see the truth."

"The truth?" Robert asked.

"Yes, the truth. Or as you called it, the other things. What truths are you wanting to be blind to?" she asked.

That was a hard question. As much as they had talked about his blindness in the afterlife being a result of his choices, the reality of it hadn't sunk in until now. Now he could see, at least to an extent, that there was a conscious choice to not look at the whole picture. The myopia his mother had spoken about was clear. Blinders. Why had he chosen that word?

He thought about the accident and its aftermath. A wave of emotion hit him and instead of giving in to the anger, he sat with it and explored it with curiosity. He remembered his emotions in the hospital and noticed something interesting. He hadn't been angry. Why had he not felt angry? There were cuts and bruises and plenty of pain, but no anger. He remembered feeling worry. Worry for Sandra and not himself. Images of bloody hands and broken glass flashed through his memory. He remembered her worry and panic for him. Strings of apologies he deftly sidestepped by telling her he was fine and focusing on her injuries. He felt the genuine care and concern he had for his younger sister and enjoyed the sensation of love, even amidst a crisis.

So where was it? When did the anger come in? What was he not seeing? He remembered going back to his home and going to sleep. Then, waking up in darkness only to learn it was mid-day. He was blind. And there was the anger. Anger grew from the seed of shock. It grew like a noxious weed, defying attempts to push it away or pull it out. The anger sunk its villainous roots into his heart, searching for something. It needed something to blame. Something to give meaning to the terrible loss. And it settled on Sandra.

Chapter 36

The Artwork

May 1984

Robert?" Heather peeked her head into the studio. "Are you in here?" She took a few steps in and looked around. She had knocked a few times without a response. That wasn't typical for Robert. Usually, he would peek out the door with a mild look of annoyance at having been interrupted. His studio was as clean and orderly as she had come to expect. What she didn't expect was to have Robert missing in the mid-afternoon. *The Garden Path* sat on the easel prominently in the middle of the room.

He really is quite good, she thought as she sat down in his chair. She admired the seamless repairs he had accomplished, brushstrokes blending perfectly with the original. She had watched him for the past couple of years at a distance, admiring his restoration skill. More than most, he had an incredible talent for not just matching colors, but restoring the feeling and life to a piece of artwork. She figured that someone who could catch the life of a painting so well must have a fascinating life of his own. So far, she'd only seen glimpses of that through his typically negative and gloomy exterior. But every time he talked about colors, something came alive inside him. Heather loved that. She was determined to get to know *that* side of Robert.

She had been thrilled that her recent promotion had increased her ability to interact with the other artists and creatives at the museum. While she loved to be in her own studio analyzing and restoring artwork, she craved more social interaction. Now she, of necessity, was interacting with many people from multiple departments. Her mother had been very pleased with that development. Now, instead of nagging her single, thirty-something-year-old daughter about getting out more, she could nag for information about all the men she was meeting. Heather rolled her eyes at the thought of her mother's inability to see her accomplishment as a professional.

What she hadn't expected was how much she enjoyed the more frequent interactions with Robert. He was an attractive man. Not the smack you in the face, gorgeous type of good looks, she wasn't really into that, and those kinds of men wouldn't really pay any attention to her anyway. Heather preferred to be subtle, like an artwork that could grab you because of the depth of its meaning and emotion, not the vibrant colors that would obnoxiously shout at your eyes and force you to look at them. So, she didn't like to be bowled over with flashy clothes, perfect hair, or the newest cologne. Robert was invested and passionate about his work. There was a depth to him that begged to be explored. He was a bit slow to pick up on her attempts to flirt with him, but she wasn't all that good at flirting anyway.

The door opened. Heather stood up quickly, feeling awkward that she was sitting, uninvited, in his office. Robert entered, the headphones over his ears connected to a Walkman clipped at his waist. He was focusing intently on some memo showing the Olympic rings. He walked directly toward her, not even looking up.

"Hi, Robert," Heather announced herself to prevent an inevitable collision.

Robert jumped, letting out a little shout. He stared at her for a moment in confusion. She watched him slowly relax as a look of familiarity showed in his countenance. "Oh, hey," Robert paused. He looked quickly over at *The Garden Path*.

"Heather," he said awkwardly. "Can I help you with something?"

"Sorry to scare you, Robert," Heather apologized. "I knocked, but you didn't answer. I thought maybe you hadn't heard me and let myself in," She felt awkward standing there having to explain herself. "The restoration is coming along beautifully," she blurted out.

"Thank you," Robert said. "It isn't as easy as I had hoped it would be. I'm sorry it's taking longer than I expected." He glanced down at the memo in his hand.

This is why she had come. Normally, this was a smooth conversation with the restorer, but this whole interaction had started the wrong way. "I see you got my memo," she said looking down at the paper in his hands.

"Yeah," came his one-word reply.

"I wanted to explain it to you before you read it because I worried you might think it was directed only at you."

"It isn't?" Robert asked.

"Well, no," Heather answered weakly. "The museum board moved up the deadline for having the gallery completed because they wanted to host a few private tours before it opens to the public," Robert just stared at her blankly. He was so difficult to read. "All the restorers and the curator have been feeling the time crunch for the exhibit and I know how hard that can be. Moving up the deadline is just more stress."

Robert just raised his eyebrows and nodded. Heather watched him walk past her over to the painting and sit down. His shoulders slumped a little and he leaned closer to inspect the repairs still needed.

"This is my favorite piece for the whole exhibit," Heather admitted. "I wanted you to know that. The mood and emotion of the light and shadow are almost magical. You're doing a brilliant job with it."

"Thank you," he said flatly. "I'll do what I can to have it done and ready for the private showings."

"I'm sure you will," Heather said, trying to encourage him. "You always do. Is there anything I can do to help?"

"I don't think so," Robert said, picking up his brushes.

"Ok, well, let me know if you think of something." She walked out of the studio. Not that she wanted to; she had hoped to be able to sit and talk with Robert for longer, but he just looked so morose that she didn't think he would want her around. The door shut behind her with a click.

Heather kicked herself for sending out the memo before talking to Robert. She was trying hard to get him to pay attention and have some interest in her, even if it was partially just to appease her mother's incessant questions. If she hadn't known Robert better, she would just think him obtuse and move on. However, she loved his passion for the artwork and the restoration process. He, more than any of the other employees, shared that love. She wished she knew how to draw his singular attention onto her.

Robert stared blankly at the canvas. One month. One month to have it completed and ready for exhibit. Factoring in paint and varnish drying times, he would need to have all the paint work done by tonight. He felt the darkness settling on him. As familiar as it was, he hated it. It sucked away his energy and motivation. He didn't have time for that.

Robert stood up and walked over to the phone and dialed the familiar numbers for his sister. This wasn't going to help his mood. She answered after a few rings with her typical bright, sunshiny voice.

"Hey, Sandra, it's Robert."

"Are you OK?" she asked. She could always sense the darkness.

"I'm fine," he lied. "I'm going to have to cancel for tonight. The deadline for this painting just changed and I'm going to have to stay late."

"Oh, Robert, we were all going to see the new Robert Redford movie together. Bobby's going to be so disappointed you aren't there," the disappointment in her voice was obvious. It weighed on him, and resentment threatened to boil up. He couldn't afford to entertain that emotion. Not now.

"I know. Tell him I'm sorry. I just lost a couple of weeks on this project because the board wants to do some private showings before the exhibit officially opens."

Robert hung up the phone and stared for a long time at *The Garden Path*. The cracks and filler shouted at him, vying for his attention, drowning out his ability to see the good work he had already done. There wasn't all that much left to finish, but what was left would still take him late into the night.

He walked out of his office. He was going to need coffee.

Chapter 37

The Incident

May 1961

T hank you, Robert," his mother said as she stepped into his room. She looked so tired. "Thank you for being there for Sandra and standing up for what's right."

"Is she OK?" Robert asked.

"She will be," she said as she sat down on Robert's bed, near his feet. "She's pretty shaken up right now though. That was traumatic. She's going to need a lot of love and care in the coming weeks."

"Mom?" Robert looked up at her, jaws clenching. "Why am I still so angry?"

"Oh, Robert," she scooted forward and grabbed his hand. "It's normal to feel angry in a situation like this. You just watched someone try to violate your sister, and then got into a fight with him. Adrenaline is probably still running through your body."

"Yeah, I guess I'm still mad at Joe, but that's not what I'm talking about," Robert said.

His mom raised her eyebrows at him. "Then what are you still angry about?" she asked.

"Dad." It was a simple answer, but the word itself stoked his emotions even further. The memory of his mother crying on the floor of her room bubbled to the surface and he squeezed her hand tighter. His father had ruined everything in their life, and there was nothing Robert could do about it.

She didn't say anything at first. Robert looked up at the pained expression on her face and felt his resentment build. "I still feel angry sometimes too," she admitted.

"I just want to find him and punch him in the face," Robert said through clenched teeth.

"And what would that accomplish?" his mother asked.

"It'd make me feel better," Robert said. He looked away from the sad look on his mother's face. Those sapphire blue eyes were penetrating, and he couldn't face them as the anger raged inside him.

"How would that make you feel better?"

"'Cause he'd get what he deserves." Robert ground his teeth.

"And then your anger would go away?"

He didn't answer. He'd imagined himself punching his dad many times. It never made the anger go away. The anger only grew, filling his heart with more resentment. What bothered him is that he liked the feeling. It was validating. He felt less impotent in this powerless situation.

"Robert," she pulled his face around to look at her with her soft hand. "It's OK to feel angry. Just don't let it turn you into an angry person. I couldn't bear to lose my sweet son."

He looked at her then. Straight into those deep eyes and decided. He would stuff these emotions deep, away from her sight. He'd do it for her. But he'd never forgive his father.

Chapter 38

The Afterlife

W hat does the anger do for you, Robert?" his mother asked him again.

It was an odd question and Robert wasn't quite sure how to answer. He had never thought about emotions doing anything for him. However, as he considered the question, he realized that in some weird way, his anger had served as a protection, or maybe even a distraction from a truth he didn't want to face.

"I'm not sure, Mom," Robert answered. "That's not something that I've thought of before. I mean, I know it makes me feel angry."

"Do you feel anything else when you're angry?"

"What do you mean?" Robert asked.

"Do you feel any other emotions when you're angry?" she asked. "Or, maybe another question to consider: What emotions do you feel that lead you to feel angry?"

Again, Robert felt overwhelmed with the depths these questions were forcing him to consider. Weren't emotions just the natural result of some situation or event? The more his mother asked the questions, the more he realized that there was more to the emotional equation than he had ever considered.

Robert reflected on his anger towards Sandra. Something had changed dramatically when he had woken blind. Why had his anger settled on her? What had he felt before the anger flooded him? It felt so immediate; like a reflex. How had anger become a reflex? And what was it a reflex for?

He focused on when he first realized that he was blind and let the experience penetrate him. Panic. Fear. Powerlessness. The emotions were intense. It was the feeling of grasping for something out of reach while falling further and further away into a pit of blackness. Nothing he could do could change the outcome. The total loss. He had no control over the situation.

"I felt powerless. I didn't have any control over my situation," Robert said.

"Hmm, yes. Those are hard things to feel," his mom said. "So, what did anger do to those emotions?"

Robert let the anger flood in. He sat with the sensations in his body and noticed the tangible change of energy. He felt a wild power. It was false control. A sense that he was in control while still being out of control.

"Anger made me powerful," Robert admitted. "I hated the feeling of not being in control. Even with a painting that was heavily damaged, I could control putting it back together and restoring it. But with the blindness, I couldn't. There was nothing I could do to change it; to bring back the tool that was so critical to my livelihood. It was this feeling of profound impotence. Anger was like a reaction to not being able to do anything about my situation. Like a hole in my life, and it filled that hole with a feeling of power."

"That's an important insight, Robert." She scooted closer to him and rested her hand on his leg. "So the lack of control in a situation is hard for you. It leads you to feel powerless."

"Yes," Robert admitted. "But it's more than that. Anger is like a resting place for the feeling of loss. And not just momentary loss, but the kind of loss that causes chain reactions that just keep resulting in more loss. I think my anger is a feeble attempt to stop the loss or to find a way to assign blame for it."

"And a way to not accept the loss and move on with a different life."

She said it simply and without accusation, but it stung. Stung with the power of truth. That was a feeling he wanted to avoid too. Her words were like a light being shined in a dark corner revealing an emaciated rat trying desperately to hide. A rat that had been gnawing away at his soul, leaving it a patchwork of ragged edges and holes.

"So why the anger at Sandra? What are you holding on to with her?" his mother asked.

Robert was ready to let it go. He was tired of the emotional cost of holding in his resentment. "It's the going through the light like I said before. If she was paying attention, she could have stopped. The car wouldn't have hit us, and I wouldn't have gone blind."

They sat in silence for a moment. Robert replayed the scene over and over in his mind like he had thousands of times before. He tried to stop the car from going into the intersection, but his mind would never let him imagine a different outcome. It always went right through that glowing yellow light where the other car could smash into him and snatch away his vision and his way of life.

"And that's what you've been telling yourself all these years?" she asked.

"That's what I experienced, Mom. I was there. I didn't make this up," Robert said, feeling defensive.

"I'm not saying you made anything up, Robert," she calmly replied. "I'm trying to bring attention to your internal narrative and understand your perspective of events."

"Yeah, well, that's what happened, so I guess that's what I've been telling myself," Robert said, sarcasm creeping into his tone.

"And what's the cost of that perspective?" Another simple question with deep implications.

Robert breathed heavily. He'd just let out something he had worked so hard to keep inside for decades, and it was immediately questioned. The temptation to shut down and push his mother away was rising in his chest. Somehow, he had thought that simply letting out what his resentment was would just make it go away. Apparently, there was more to it.

"I can see it in you even now," his mother responded to the silence. "It's a determination toward bitterness and depression. Can you see how that perspective is destroying your peace and happiness? And yet you're afraid to consider another perspective, a perspective that might allow you to see the joy and beauty that still exists in the world."

"What's this other perspective you keep talking about, Mom?" Robert asked. "You seem to think that there was something else that happened, and I'm just not seeing it."

"That's because you're blind, son. You refuse to see."

"Tell me then, because I really don't get this other perspective you're saying exists." He was trying hard to stay open, but this event had defined so much of how he had viewed his world for a major portion of his life.

"Let me ask you another question," she said. "When you had your vision, did you ever drive through a yellow light?"

"Yes, of course," Robert answered quickly.

"And how many accidents did you get in doing so?"

He sensed a trap. "None."

"So, you're trying to tell me that when Sandra did something that you had done many times in your life, without any accidents, that suddenly the accident was her fault?"

Robert was surprised at the energy she was putting into the question. He paused to think about the logic she was presenting. It was a logic he had refused to consider the many times it had crept into his consciousness. He needed something to blame. Some target to place his loss of control and independence on. Somehow, he had grasped at a yellow light and found that to be logical.

"Robert," she said, her voice calmer, "if the light had been red, like the person's light was who crashed into you, then I could understand your perspective a little. But you're holding on to a memory that you've poisoned with accusation. Your need to place blame created a more damaging blindness than the accident itself ever did."

She was right. It hurt to admit it, but it was true. This bitterness had sullied the sweetness of connection he had felt towards his sister. Sure, he still cared about her and appreciated the things she did for him, but it was always through the filter of blame.

"I'm a fool." He stopped for a moment. The heavy implications of this truth attacked his defenses, breaking down barriers and leaving humility. "How could I have been so stupid and short-sighted?" Robert pulled at his hair as anxiety attacked his senses.

His mother stayed quiet, letting him wrestle with the perspective shift. Robert stood up and tried to walk around, but the fresh darkness caused him to stumble and trip to the ground. He punched the ground in frustration.

"Why couldn't I see how ridiculous that rationale was?"

Again, there was no response. No encouraging words to benumb his realization. She was going to make him do the work. He exhaled, releasing tension he hadn't even noticed. He had to face this.

"I guess I needed control. I couldn't stop it from happening, so I focused on the yellow light because that's all I saw. I didn't see the other car coming. I needed to blame my blindness on something because I couldn't bear to accept the rest of my life without sight."

"So you chose to live a visionless life without sight."

It hadn't been a question. A simple statement of fact. And he could see it now. He had withheld love and forgiveness and prevented himself from feeling it from others. The accident hadn't been Sandra's fault. She'd been just as much of a victim as he had. Actually, more. She'd had to endure years of his coldness each time she sought his forgiveness. He had never given that to her, because of his blindness.

"This isn't the only time you've done this, Robert," she continued. "Your sight has been limited for much longer than the accident."

"What do you mean?" he asked.

"This thing that you did with Sandra, blaming her for all your problems in your life, isn't the first time you've done that. You've used resentment as a shield, preventing you from seeing the joy and beauty around you before."

Robert felt his heart tighten. He thought he knew what she was talking about, but he asked anyway. "When?"

"I think you need someone else to answer that question," she answered.

"Who?"

A deep voice sounded from the right of his mother. "Hi, Robert."

Chapter 39

The Incident

July 1961

The summer sun shined brightly on her face as she sipped iced tea on the front lawn. She needed this. One of her first days off from work in several weeks. She felt the strain of two jobs draining her reserves of energy and focus. She knew her children were missing her. Needing her. But today, they both were working at their own jobs, and the laundry was already done. So, she was going to relax and recuperate.

She looked down the street of cookie-cutter homes and marveled at the facade of sameness. There was no doubt that the neighbors knew her husband had left her, and she was alone with her two kids. No one talked to her about it though. No offers of support. Just sideways glances and whispered conversations. Exactly what she didn't need. She would show them though. Show them that this woman was steady; resilient. She would show them a smiling face and a positive spirit to cover the exhaustion, shame, sadness, and loneliness that threatened the threads of her sanity.

But today was a good day, and she was going to enjoy it. The mailman rounded the corner down the street and progressed from house to house, toting a heavy bag at his side. She wondered if he had a family, and if so, how he treated his kids. She imagined him coming home from a long day of walking the streets and collapsing on the floor, surrounded by laughing children vying for his attention. Pangs of sadness and hurt swelled in her chest.

No. She was not going to go there today. It was her day off and she was going to enjoy it, not wallow in gloom. Wiping away the beginning of a tear, she put a smile back on her face and greeted the mailman with warmth.

"Good afternoon, Frank," she beamed. "Such a lovely day, isn't it?"

"A bit hot to be out on the street all day, but who's complaining?" he smiled back at her. "I've got a few things for you today, Mrs. Martin."

He pulled out several envelopes from his bag and handed them to her. Most looked like bills; however, one was thicker than the rest, and "Helen" was written clearly across the front in very familiar handwriting. She had seen many envelopes like this during the war. Each had made her heart flutter with excitement. However, today, it had a very different effect.

"Have a nice day, Mrs. Martin," the mailman almost sang as he continued down the street.

She tried her best to ignore the *Mrs.* that the mailman repeated. It was a reminder of what wasn't. A reminder like the one staring up at her, heavy in her hand. They weren't divorced, so technically the title was still accurate, but up until today, Helen figured she would never hear from him again. She stared at the letters spelling out her name for a long time. The writing was pressed deep into the paper. He was still haunted by the past, she could tell. His fleeing their home had not been an escape.

Helen walked inside with the mail. She wouldn't be able to enjoy the sunshine with that letter. Keeping her happy mask on when she opened it would likely be impossible. Carefully, she slid her finger under the flap and gently tore an opening at the top of the envelope.

A single piece of paper was wrapped around a stack of cash. Helen's hand went instinctively to her mouth as she realized the bills were mostly twenties and fifties. Pulling the cash from the paper revealed a single line of writing. "I'm sorry," it said. She turned the paper over, looking for any other writing or explanation. There was nothing.

Helen's emotions bounced back and forth between gratitude, shock, and betrayal as she counted the money. Five hundred dollars. Wherever he was, he was earning money and living life. Why did he need to leave? Why couldn't he be working at home with his family and providing for their needs? She had so many questions, each with a litany of emotions ready to flood her senses.

The envelope had no return address. Even the post office's processing stamp was smeared and gave no indication of where her husband had gone. The only thing she had heard from him in almost six months was two simple words: I'm sorry. Well, as far as she was concerned, that would not earn her forgiveness. He had turned their life upside down and he thought a little note with five hundred dollars would fix that? No, sir. Sure, the money would help. In fact, it would cover what they were lacking for Robert's first year's tuition and then some.

This was all too much. She couldn't handle the rollercoaster of emotions. Too many questions and not enough answers. Helen walked to her room and grabbed the newspaper she kept hidden beneath the mattress. There had to be answers there.

Dinner had been quiet with Sandra. Helen couldn't seem to maintain the smile she usually wore. Financially, she felt relief, but she was emotionally exhausted. Just when she was starting to move on and get in a rhythm, that letter had to show up and disrupt everything. Sandra could tell something was off; she kept looking up and asking if everything was OK. Thankfully, Sandra had stopped pressing the issue and left to go out with her friends. Helen needed to prepare for Robert to get home.

It was after eleven when he quietly opened the front door. Helen watched him take off his shoes and walk carefully towards his room.

"How was work tonight, Robert?"

Robert jumped. "Jeez, Mom, you scared me. I told you, you don't need to stay up for me."

"I know," she answered as she fingered the stack of cash she was holding under the table. "There's just something I need to share with you, and I couldn't wait until morning."

The boy stopped and looked at her with concern written on his face. He had grown up so much these last six months. So much of his spark for life had faded as he tried his best to take on the weight of his family's needs. Helen felt a swell of emotions spinning in her chest.

"What is it, Mom?" Robert asked, stepping toward her. "Is everything alright?"

"Yes, everything's fine," she lied. "Come, sit down with me."

He obeyed, never taking his eyes off her. "Are you sure, Mom? You look really tired. Something happened, didn't it?"

"Yes, something happened, but it's a good thing," she said as she pulled out the cash and set it on the top of the table. She didn't explain but just looked into his eyes, trying to read his expression.

"How much is it?" Robert asked.

"Five hundred."

"Where did it come from?"

This was the point Helen had struggled with for hours. What should she tell this boy? They needed the money, that was without doubt. However, this boon came with a heavy shadow. A shadow that if Robert knew about, she was sure he would reject it entirely. She didn't want to lie to him, but she didn't want to tell him the truth either.

"It was an anonymous donation." It wasn't a lie. He hadn't written his name anywhere on the envelope or note. Just because she recognized the handwriting didn't mean he had told them it was from him, right? Helen tried to put on her best smile. "This will cover the rest of the costs for your first year in Chicago."

Robert eyed her. "An anonymous donation? Where did you get it?"

"It came in the mail. The mailman gave it to me this afternoon," she could see he was skeptical. "Isn't this wonderful?"

"It's a lot of money," Robert picked up the pile and began counting it. Helen watched the gears in his head turning as he got to the last bill. "Well, at least *someone* is watching out for us."

His words were dripping with meaning. Someone other than his dad. Her heart ached for this boy of hers. If he knew where the money had come from, he would reject it. If only he could understand that it was the best his father could do for him right now. If only she could heal that deep wound in his heart. But it wasn't hers to heal.

The Afterlife

The deep, quiet gristly voice startled Robert. When had someone else shown up? Then, almost as soon as the shock wore off, emotions began filling his heart. Anger, bitterness, sadness, confusion, and surprisingly—longing. It was more than he could handle. He started opening his mouth to say something, but he had no words. All these years of thinking about what he would say to this man if he ever met him again, and now he couldn't say anything.

"Robert, before you say anything, there's something I need to say first." The sound of his father's voice triggered so many memories. "I'm sorry. I know I caused you a lot of hurt and pain and I am sorry for that, son."

He couldn't respond. He had wanted to hear those words. To feel them heal the anger and sadness that always seemed to brew deep in his heart. To see this man who had abandoned him. Abandoned his mom and his sister. He had wanted to have him return to their lives and take up the role that he so easily walked away from. But now, painfully, the words just felt empty to him. He couldn't see his father standing there beside him. He couldn't look into his eyes and see if he was sincere or not.

"Why?" It was all Robert could muster to say.

"I don't want to feed you excuses, Robert," his dad said softly. "What I did was wrong, and I'm sorry."

"You ruined my life, Dad. I think you can at least tell me why." Robert's heart was beating hard now, and he could feel the heat of years of pent-up anger and resentment rising.

"Robert," his mother interjected, placing her hand on his shoulder.

"No, Mom," Robert shrugged off her hand. "I have every right to be angry at this man."

"Helen, I knew this wasn't a good idea," Robert's father said, his voice disappointed.

"John," Helen said forcefully, "you stay right here." Robert had no memory of his mother ever speaking to his father that way. "This is exactly what he needs right now, even if he hates every second of it. He's blind and he hasn't been willing to face your part in that. So, you will stay, and you will help your son through this challenge. You might even do some healing yourself."

There was a profound silence. When had his mother developed such a commanding presence? The censure was directed at his father, but Robert felt it himself. The message was clear; you are being immature. You are holding on to something that is impacting your sight and it is time to start letting go. Robert bowed his head. It was too much. How could he face this? How could he survive the barrage of thoughts and emotions that he had so deftly stuffed away for so many years?

"John," his mother interrupted the silence. "I believe he asked you for an explanation."

Robert heard a deep exhale. "OK," came his deep voice, "I'll try. Robert, you may as well sit down; this is going to take a while." Robert heard his father sit down in the grass next to him.

He fought back the stubbornness to stay standing and sat down. His mother sat down next to him and placed her hand on his knee. It had a calming effect, though he could still feel a hardness in his heart towards his father.

"Again," his father started, "the most important thing I can say is that I'm sorry. I don't want to make any excuses for my behavior. What I did was wrong, and I'm sorry it had such a big impact on your life." There was silence again for a moment.

"Robert, the war did things to me. It did things to a lot of people, but it changed me. My mind was sick. I was against the war from the moment the United States got involved. I always looked at war as a death machine, but my biggest problem was how it made good men do bad things out of desperation. We should never have to be in a situation where our choice is to kill or be killed.

"In boot camp, I saw my friends change. The way they started talking about the Germans and the Japanese sickened me. They clumped whole groups of people into a faceless enemy that needed to be killed. The drill instructors wanted to beat out independent thought and make murderers out of us. Automatons that would kill on command. I couldn't escape it either. The shame of leaving the military was so high that I knew my life would be ruined if I returned home early."

"What about the shame of leaving your family?" Robert asked.

"Robert, just listen," his mother interjected, squeezing his leg.

"No, Helen," his father spoke up, "that's a fair question. Robert, you're right, what I did was shameful. In my defense though, by then my mind was so sick I couldn't see through the fog and smoke of my trauma. I thought about coming back to you so many times, but I was paralyzed with panic. Images of the war would flood my mind and threaten my sanity.

"Robert, I saw terrible things in the war. I saw men do terrible things to each other, and all because someone had commanded them to march against each other. I did terrible things, and all because I'd been trained to blindly follow orders. I was a pawn in someone else's sickening chess game. Those images haunted me, and I couldn't forgive myself for the things I'd done."

"But why did you leave us, Dad?" Robert asked. "We weren't at war anymore. Everything was fine. Our life was good, and then you left and ruined that." Robert had heard of the effects of war. He'd seen the boys come back from Vietnam with haunted looks on their faces. But he didn't know what they had gone through. As much as he wanted to understand his father's experience in the war, it still didn't explain the sudden, inexplicable abandonment during a time of peace.

"Again, Robert, I'm sorry for that. It pains me to know that I hurt you so much. Everything I'm saying just feels like an excuse. Helen, I don't think this is going to work."

"Keep talking, John."

John exhaled deeply. It took a moment for him to resume his narrative. "I tried to keep my flashbacks away from you and your sister. I avoided talking about anything that could be related to the war. I never even talked to your mother about it. Everything was just too painful. I wanted to rid myself of that terrible experience. But I couldn't. Each day was a battle.

"I would see the faces of my dead company members at work. I would see them in crowds. A darkness was settling over my mind; a darkness that had begun while I was away at war. Shadows stalked me and I tried to ignore them. I tried to act natural, like nothing was happening. But it was eating away at my sanity. I tried to put on a normal face for you Robert, but inside I was tormented."

"Why didn't you get help, Dad?" Robert asked.

"Can I ask you a question first, Robert?" his dad asked.

Robert hesitated. "This isn't about me, Dad."

"I think it is, Robert. It's all about you. We aren't having this conversation for my benefit; despite what your mother tells me it will do for me. We're talking because you're blind and need your sight restored. I've gone through hell to heal from my mental sickness. I've struggled to forgive myself for the things in my life. I imagine I still have work to do there. But right now, Robert, this conversation is for you, not me. So will you answer me a question before I answer yours?"

"I guess," Robert relented.

"Why didn't *you* get help with your trauma and depression?"

The question slammed into Robert. His whole life he had avoided talking to anyone about his issues. Even when talking with a therapist had stopped being so taboo, Robert avoided the suggestion from his mother and Sandra. He hadn't wanted to seem weak. There was something about talking to a professional about his problems that just screamed *incapable*. And yet, here he was criticizing his dad for not doing the very thing he had been unwilling to do for himself. He didn't want to face that truth, so he did what came naturally; he deflected.

"What do you know of my trauma and depression?"

"Robert," his father started, "there's a lot you don't know about me. And one of the first of those things is how much I care about you. I was terrible at showing it in life, but you and your sister are what kept me going so much of the time."

"Then why did you leave us?" Robert retorted quickly.

"Because I was sick. My mind was broken. That's what I've been trying to tell you. What I did wasn't rational. It was wrong, and I'm sorry for it. I tried in my own way to make up for it, but I know it wasn't enough."

"What did you ever do to make up for leaving us? We never heard from you again."

The question weighed heavily in the air. "Helen, you never told him?"

"If he knew, he wouldn't have accepted it," Helen explained, a twinge of defensiveness in her voice. "He was so bitter towards you that even the mention of you put a dark cloud over him for days."

"What are you guys talking about?" Robert asked. "Tell me about what?"

"Helen, why don't you tell him now?"

Robert felt his mother's hand take his own. She squeezed it as she always did before talking to him about something serious. He squeezed back letting her know it was OK to tell him whatever it was that she had kept from him all those years ago.

"Robert," she started, "the first time I heard back from your dad was the summer right before you went to college."

"The first time?" Robert asked, surprised. "You mean you heard from him more than once? Why didn't you tell me, Mom?"

"Like I just told your dad, you were still so angry that I knew you wouldn't accept what he was giving. But you, we, needed it so bad."

"What did he give? I never saw anything."

"Yes, you did. I showed it to you the day it arrived. It's what got you through your first year of college."

Realization hit Robert. The money. The anonymous five hundred dollars. It hadn't been anonymous. His mom was right; had he known that was from his father, he would have refused it. The wound of the abandonment was still too fresh back then. For some reason, it felt fresh even now.

"There were other times?" Robert asked his mother, starting to connect more dots.

"Every year I got an envelope in the mail, written in his hand with another five hundred dollars in it. Each time the money was wrapped with a simple note saying I'm sorry."

Robert turned toward his dad. "I don't get it. None of this makes any sense to me. Why would you abandon us out of the blue and then send money? You say you cared. You wrote notes saying you were sorry. Why not just come back to us?"

"I know it doesn't make any sense," his dad started, voice slow and deep. "Now that I've had lots of time to start healing here, I can see that more clearly. But at the time, it was the only thing I could think of. My mind was frayed. I'd lost touch with reality, and I couldn't see the safety I was living in each day. So many things felt like a threat to me. Internally, I was so close to my snapping point. The only thing that kept me rooted in reality was you, and Sandra."

"Again," Robert said in exasperation, "that doesn't make any sense. If we were the only things that kept you rooted in reality, why did you leave us?"

His father breathed out slowly. "The day I left, I'd been reading the newspaper as usual before I left for work. You and Sandra had already left for school. I came across an article reporting that Eisenhower had severed diplomatic relationships with Cuba. I knew that was the first step that would lead us back into war. I could see myself being forced to kill people again. My mind snapped. I couldn't do it again. I had to escape.

"The whole time I was away at war, I fantasized that I had fled to Canada instead of enlisting. It was the escape my mind had created to flee the terrors I was witnessing. So, with the threat in my mind of having to go back into that nightmare, I knew I had to go to Canada. Nothing could stop me. I packed my stuff, got in the car, and drove to the border."

Emotions were storming within Robert. Empathy kept swirling to the surface, and it bothered him how difficult it was to stay angry. He had lived through the Vietnam draft. While he was just a couple of months too old to be drafted, he had still felt the pressures and judgments from those being sent off to war. Vietnam had been a very unpopular war, and many had fled the country to avoid the draft. Robert knew he would have been tempted to do so as well. Now he was learning that this was what his dad had done to flee a war that he never would have been called to serve in. He wished he could have looked into his dad's eyes and seen the pain there. To see him from an adult perspective.

He wished he'd known his father had been in the war. How much would have changed if he could have seen his dad as a war survivor? The blank stares and the far-off looks had always just been a tired man after a long day at work. Whenever Sandra had climbed into his lap, a smile would return to his face, so Robert never suspected the horrors that were behind them.

Yet, the internal battle raged on. Robert had needed a father, especially during his senior year. He had needed the strength he had assumed was always there. He still wanted to be angry at what was taken from him. But a different picture had been placed in his mind and it was impossible to ignore, as much as he wanted to.

"I'll understand if you don't forgive me, Robert," his dad said, interrupting him from his thoughts. "I never could in life. It was hard enough to do so here, even when my mind started to heal."

This struck Robert with another wave of intensity. He knew intimately what it was like to not forgive, but he had struggled to forgive someone else, not himself. Questions filled his mind, both for his father and for himself.

"Why couldn't you forgive yourself?" Robert asked, relaxing the tension in his muscles.

"I knew I'd abandoned you and your mom. I knew you needed me. But I couldn't stop, and I couldn't go back. I was stuck in a painful limbo I couldn't escape. Every morning I woke up knowing that I was a terrible person. Every morning I recommitted to living as scanty of an existence as possible so I could send as much money as I could for you and Sandra to go to college.

"After six years of doing that, I figured you both had probably finished and were able to live successfully on your own. I still hated myself for what I had done. So, one morning, I finally gave myself the consequence I felt I deserved."

Robert felt his whole body tense. It was like watching a video of a train wreck. He didn't want to hear what his dad was going to say but couldn't stop himself from needing to hear it as well.

"Killing myself didn't take away the mental torture like I thought it would. Healing, especially mental pain, takes time. It takes effort and courage. I've been facing those pains and battling them for many years now. Fortunately, I've had lots of support. Your mom has really helped me. I'm not sure how she forgave me for leaving her, but it helped my healing more than she could imagine."

"Forgiving you was a part of facing and healing my own pain," Robert's mother said, softly.

"Dad, why did you kill yourself?" Robert was shocked. He wasn't sure what to feel now.

"Because I couldn't live with the nightmares and what I had done to my family." He said it so matter-of-factly.

Robert's heart swelled within him. He had contemplated suicide so many times throughout his life. After Mary had betrayed him, the darkness that washed over him had threatened his existence. But Sandra had swept in and shined a bright light through the clouds of gloom. He realized she had been there for him in precisely the way he had needed, right when he needed it.

Had she not convinced him to go to California and live with her and Tom, Robert would have killed himself too.

Then there was the accident. Blindness had been a burden too heavy to bear. Darkness had returned two-fold. And who had been there to lift him out of the seemingly perpetual gloom? Sandra. And Tom. And Bobby. They did so despite his bitterness and coldness. And in doing so, they had saved his life from himself.

Robert started to cry. It was slow at first but progressed to great, heaving sobs. Emotions poured out of him like water breaking through a dam. Years of pent-up emotions, ignored and stuffed away, spilled through his eyes, and shook out through trembling shoulders. The log jam of bitterness and short-sightedness couldn't hold against such a flood.

Strong arms reached out and pulled Robert up into an embrace. He melted into it as he continued to sob. This was what he had missed. What he had needed. He needed his dad to hold him tight when he had felt weak. Needed to be strengthened instead of having to be strong. Robert hugged him back. He let his love pour past the hurt and into the father he had missed so much. They stood there, holding each other, for what seemed like a much-needed eternity.

"I love you, Robert," his dad said, finally breaking the silence.

"I love you too, Dad." Robert was surprised to feel his father begin to shake.

"You were right, Helen," John choked out through a broken and weepy voice. "There was more healing for me. Thank you, Robert. That means more to me than you can even imagine."

Robert opened his eyes and light poured in. There was his dad, eyes red from emotion, looking at him with a gruff smile spread across his thin lips. And then, the clearest image he had seen in twenty-five years blurred in an instant. He blinked away the tears furiously to bring back that gloriously clear picture of his dad smiling before him. As the tears streamed down his cheeks, the clarity returned. He could see.

Chapter 41

The Artwork

May 1984

R obert had dealt with deadlines before. They were a common part of the restoration process. However, it wasn't common for the date to be moved forward by two weeks. Robert stewed on that as he sipped the piping hot coffee and stared down the remaining work on *The Garden Path*. It was a beautiful painting, but right now, missing out on going to the movies with Sandra, Tom, and Bobby made it feel more like a burden. He was going to have to get over that.

He had come to the focal point of the painting. A well-dressed couple walked the path and stood in the singularly illuminated spot of the piece. Robert had put off this section several times during the process. He wasn't sure why, but he felt nervous about messing it up. Normally he would have started the painting process at the focal point. Cracks ran through the man and woman and up through the beam of light shining on them. Robert studied the brushwork to understand how the artist painted it.

Satisfied, Robert began mixing the paint. As he pulled whites and pinks together onto his pallet, a smile began to spread, relaxing the tension in his shoulders. Color was his dearest friend. He loved the magic and illusion it could create by simply blending and placing it in the right places. The stress of the new deadline melted away as Robert repaired the woman's glowing white dress.

Minutes turned to hours as Robert poured himself into the work. He enjoyed each stroke with the satisfaction of the final piece to a thousand-piece puzzle. Standing back, Robert admired the work. Save for one last portion he had saved for the end, it was done. He imagined what it had been like for Adenet Dupuis to step back from his finished painting. It was beautiful. The composition and color flowed so well with the texture of each brushstroke. This was what Robert loved about his job. To bring back to life the beauty of such masterworks was a rich reward.

He had saved the man in the painting until the end. He didn't know why, but it seemed fitting somehow. Maybe it was the dream of a meaningful relationship that he felt was too distant and impossible. Maybe it was the fear of yet another broken heart. For some reason, Robert had placed himself in that collection of well-placed brushstrokes. It was time to finish it.

He mixed a black that was not really black, but a dark highlight of blue made alive by the light of the sun. With a few strokes, it was done. It was no longer recognizable from the blackened, smokey mess that had arrived at his office months ago. Now, it was a ray of hope and love, like the sunbeam stretching down through the trees. Robert smiled.

The Afterlife

Robert was shocked at the change in his heart. There was a lightness there that he couldn't remember ever feeling before. Looking around, he basked in the beauty of heaven. Emerald greens, sapphire blues, alizarin crimson; the beauty of it flooded him with joy. His mother stood there smiling at him as she wiped tears from her cheeks. Robert's heart filled with gratitude for this incredible woman.

"Let's go for a walk," his mother suggested. She placed her hand in the crook of his elbow and led him forward. His father followed on his other side. It was the happiest he could ever remember feeling. This surprised him standing next to the person he had focused so much of his bitterness and anger on.

"Robert," his father said, "I'm sorry I wasn't there for you throughout your life. I wish I had been."

Robert stopped and looked into his father's eyes. "Dad, I've spent so much of my life angry at the pain you caused me. I can't even begin to explain all my bitterness, but I don't want to anymore. I didn't understand what you'd gone through. I only saw my own pain." The words that he knew he needed to say, and should have said long ago, came quickly to his lips. "I forgive you."

His father smiled a deep, relieved smile. It seemed to Robert that his features became just a little brighter and clearer. They embraced again. "Thank you, Robert. It's not deserved, so

I'll receive it as a gift. I've learned that forgiveness is a gift that heals both ways. I love you."

Robert felt the truth of that statement. He *saw* the truth of that statement. Letting go of his bitterness and anger toward his father had freed him from a dark, emotional prison. It allowed the light of love and gratitude to pour into his heart.

"Robert?" his mother asked. "What are you noticing?

"That I suffered a much more debilitating blindness than losing my vision," Robert reflected. "I couldn't see or appreciate all the good and love that was so present in the people in my life."

"Yes, and now that you can see it?"

"I was a fool."

"We all are, to one degree or another. The sooner we realize it, the quicker we can heal from that malady." Her face was so beautiful and serene. No trace of the pain he had grown so accustomed to seeing before she passed away.

"Thank you, Mom, for opening my eyes to it."

"What about the accident? Any change in your perspective there?"

Robert focused on the transformation in his heart. There were so many new feelings there. One small feeling, tucked away in the corner, tugged at his attention. Regret. Regret that he had not forgiven Sandra in life. Regret that he had not given her that gift. With that emotion came the recognition that she had never deserved the condemnation he had held to.

"It was wrong of me not to forgive Sandra," Robert said. "She only ever tried to serve me and loved me more than I ever deserved. She blessed and saved my life on so many occasions. I don't know if I ever would have realized that if I hadn't learned your story, Dad."

"My story?" His father looked genuinely surprised. "How did my story help you?"

"I almost committed suicide several times. And Sandra was always there when I needed someone the most. I don't feel any anger towards her anymore. I just wish that I had told her that in life."

"You'll get a chance to tell her when she arrives here. It will be a part of your continued healing, and hers," his mother said. "Remember, Robert, heaven isn't a place for bitterness and regret. It's a place for love and unity. As we all heal and learn from the challenges and weaknesses of mortality, we realize that more and more."

"Yeah," Robert said, "I'm starting to see that. Forgiving you, Dad has filled me with so much joy. I never would have expected that."

"The feeling is mutual," his dad said.

They continued walking together. Robert marveled at the beauty and perfection around him. Gratitude flooded his heart as he watched the trees sway in the slight breeze. The sun shined through branches, creating dancing patterns of light and shadow where they walked. He basked in the vibrancy of it all. This was what he had missed.

"Robert," his mother interrupted the silence, "life takes a toll on all of us. You went through so many challenging things. As a mother, it was hard to watch you deal with those things, both while I was on Earth, and from here."

Robert listened. He never experienced being a parent, so he couldn't fully understand her perspective. However, he imagined the love he felt for Bobby and how much he appreciated being a part of his life.

"You still have some significant pain to heal to be able to experience the fullness of heaven," his mother said.

"Oh?" Robert said, surprised. He was so full of the love and gratitude he was feeling that he couldn't feel any lingering pain or sadness. "And what is that?"

"Mary."

She was right. The moment she said it, he could feel how deep that pain was. He had ignored it so much in life that he couldn't see the effect it had on him. Yet, now, without the heaviness of resentment pressing upon him, he could see it clearly. He avoided any kind of romantic relationship. He didn't trust anyone's expressed affection towards him. It left a void in his heart that he had just grown accustomed to.

"Yes," Robert acknowledged. "She really hurt me. I don't know if I can forgive what she did to me. There's no excuse for it."

"True. It was wrong," she agreed. "It was so hard to see you go through that betrayal. I was really mad at Mary for a long time."

"I don't think I ever felt mad at her," Robert admitted. "I loved her so much that I don't think I ever could have felt mad. I felt lucky and amazed that she would have taken interest in me. She was so beautiful and sweet. When I found out that she was cheating on me, I was crushed. I couldn't believe it. But I wasn't mad. I just felt incredibly insecure."

"What were you insecure about?" she asked.

"So many things," Robert answered. "Insecure that I was a bad lover. Insecure about whether she actually ever liked me or if she was just using me for something. That maybe I wasn't attractive enough to sustain her attention. I don't know, Mom. I just questioned so many things about myself. It sounds stupid now, but I blamed myself for her infidelity."

Helen raised her eyebrows in surprise. John stopped and took Robert by the shoulders. "Robert, you can't blame yourself for others' actions. That would be like you blaming yourself for my abandonment."

"Yes," Helen interrupted. "But I did that after you left. I couldn't find any other logical reason that you would have left us so suddenly. I eventually realized it wasn't my fault, but it took me a while."

John closed his mouth as he was about to say something. He just nodded instead and looked deeply at the woman he had hurt all those years ago. Robert could tell that his father still struggled with the guilt. He was surprised by the compassion he felt towards him. Robert had hurt others, too, and knew of that pain.

"John, you know I've forgiven you," Helen reassured him. "Robert needs to know that it's normal for people to blame themselves for things that aren't their fault. Sometimes it's easier to blame yourself than to accept that the person you love is flawed. I don't know why, but that was my experience."

Robert thought about what his mother was saying. There had been many moments throughout his life that his mind had started to see the fault in Mary, but he stopped himself with his negative self-talk. He would spiral into the, "If only I had been more attractive, then she would have been satisfied with just me," or "If only I had paid her more attention, then she would still be with me" statements. He could see now that these beliefs had just maintained his insecurity.

"Mom, what helped you to forgive Dad and stop blaming yourself?" Robert asked. He was struggling with the thought of forgiving Mary because it felt like telling her that what she did was OK.

"Hmm, good question," she answered, looking at John. "The first step for me was actually accepting that it wasn't my fault. I know that may seem strange, but I had to fully accept that it was him and not me."

"Why?" Robert asked.

"Well, because until I did, I was creating a false forgiveness in my head that was based on explaining away and excusing his behaviors because they must have been a result of my actions." She maintained eye contact with John and gave him a compassionate smile. "So, I wasn't actually forgiving him."

Robert reflected on that. He realized he had done much the same thing with Mary. He had tried to make things work again on the premise that he was the one who needed to change. His so-called forgiveness of her infidelity wasn't forgiveness at all. It was excusing her behavior and taking ownership of it on himself. He could see the flaw in that thinking.

"OK, I can see that," Robert said. "So, what did you do next?"

"Well, letting go of the blame allowed me to feel the anger and hurt. I got lost in that for a while," she paused, reflecting. "That's when I started to blame all my difficulties on him. As much as I put a smile on for others, I would go to pretty dark places in my head. Getting the money helped soften my heart a little, but I even found ways to be mad about that. Sometimes it just felt more like a reminder that he wasn't there supporting me than it was a boon. When it stopped coming, I felt a mix of worry and relief."

"Relief?" John asked, a pained expression on his face.

"My heart only has love for you now, John. But Robert needs to understand my process."

"I guess I do too," he said.

"Yes, I felt relief," Helen explained. "And the relief was that I wasn't getting that reminder that you weren't there by my side—that there was a painful hole in my life. Sometimes it seemed that right around the time I was coming to terms and accepting your dad's absence, that money would come and bring all those emotions back."

"I'm sorry," John said. "That isn't what I was trying to do." He reached over and touched her arm softly.

"I know," Helen answered. "And I forgive you. I didn't have the same perspective then that I do now. I had to learn that those feelings of anger and betrayal were a prison for me, and not for you," she explained as she looked back at John.

Those words resonated with Robert. He felt that prison intimately. It kept him away from relationships and love. Away from the trust for others and love for himself. He had felt trapped, and sadly, those feelings had kept him trapped in so many other situations in his life. Yet, he couldn't see a way out.

"So, how did you let go? How did you get out of the prison?" Robert asked.

"That's an interesting question. How did I let go? Well, I guess I had to figure out why I was holding on," she answered. "I had to realize that there was something about me that was needing to hold on to that pain and resentment for some reason."

"And what was it? What did you figure out?" Robert asked.

"Fairness was a part of it. The situation wasn't fair. It wasn't fair that I was a single mom and had to get a job and work myself ragged. It wasn't fair that my children didn't have their dad there to support them in ways that I couldn't. It wasn't fair that people judged me and looked down on me. And all that unfairness let me feel justified for all my failures and mistakes.

It kept me from accepting life on life's terms and moving forward.

"I didn't want it to be true. I still wanted to have the life I had imagined. Letting go of that felt like letting go of a dream; of a possibility for something better. However, I could only see one option, and it was the one that wasn't available to me anymore. So I held on tightly to the unfairness of it; barbs and prison bars and all."

"So, how did you let go?" Robert asked again.

"Sadly, it wasn't until I was here that I was able to let go. I had blamed all my pain on things that were outside of my control. When I arrived here, and still felt the pain, I had to deal with the truth that I had been holding on to something I didn't need to." She paused for a moment and reflected. "I guess it was the unfairness of still being in pain on the other side of mortality that forced me to deal with my part of it."

"I can relate to that," Robert murmured.

"Me too," his father whispered. "Me too."

"I've come to realize that most people here come holding on to something and are surprised by how the consequences of doing so fly in the face of their perception of what heaven is supposed to be. Heaven is not a free pass to healing and love. Those are things that can only come through cultivation. The joy of heaven is a reward for the work we have put into making it that way."

They sat quietly together for a moment. Robert took in the richness of his surroundings. Everything looked like a perfectly manicured botanical garden. The trees created patterns of contrasting colors with a depth Robert had never experienced in life. Flowers and shrubs blanketed the ground, creating a fresh, sweet, and earthy smell. The path they had been walking was gentle and meandering; no straight lines of rigid urgency.

Robert brought his attention to his heart and explored the emotions and self-inflicted defenses and guards. It felt much different than it had when he arrived. There was a lightness there that he couldn't remember ever feeling in life. He looked at his father while maintaining the awareness on his heart. The bitterness was gone. In its place were compassion and love.

Forgiveness had softened so much of the angst that had taken up permanent residence there.

Pressing his awareness deeper into his heart, Robert explored his thoughts and feelings towards Mary. There he found a defensive wall blocking emotions from either going in or out. Maintaining his focus on that spot, Robert felt a powerful longing behind it. It pulsed much like the physical beating of his heart. He remembered the feelings he had locked away so many years ago; the need to feel loved, and to love in return. The need for intimate companionship that had become so unsafe was still strong behind that barrier. The sensation scared Robert. As much as he wanted and needed it back, the idea of it still took him back to all the pain and hurt of Mary's betrayal.

"I'm still not sure how to let go," Robert admitted.

"More importantly right now is knowing why you are holding on," his mother said.

"I think it's protection from pain," Robert said. "I couldn't bear being hurt that way again. So, I prevented myself from ever being hurt by not allowing myself to feel that deeply anymore."

"And what's the cost of doing so?" she asked.

Robert thought for a moment before answering. "Intimacy," he realized. "Depth of companionship. As much as I had people in my life, I lived it alone."

"Is it worth the cost?"

"I keep asking myself a different question," Robert said. "Was the intimacy worth the pain?"

"Absolutely." Robert was surprised to hear his father speak up. He had been so quiet, allowing his mother to guide the conversation. His answer was bold and definitive. "I spent the last years of my life running away from the most important people in my life because of pain and hurt. And I can tell you, the pain of intimacy lost, the hole that exists in your heart, is not worth it. Intimacy is what makes life meaningful. Makes it worth living."

The weight of those last words pressed upon Robert's mind. His father's suicide had been an uncomfortable revelation for him that had shifted his thinking towards the man. Now, the perspective of life lost in an absence of intimacy challenged Robert's worldview. He realized he still had intimacy, just not to the depth he had experienced with Mary, and not romantic in any way. Always holding back had kept Robert's relationships with others superficial.

"Loss and pain are a part of life," Robert's mother interrupted him out of his thinking. "They provide a contrast that sweetens love and connection even more. Without those times, we wouldn't be able to experience a full depth of joy. Pain serves a purpose."

"But why did I have to hurt so much?" Robert asked. He felt childish with the question as he could hear the immaturity in its tone. However, it was a real question that he had asked himself throughout his life. He wasn't trying to avoid all pain, just the unbearable pain.

"Emotion and feelings are like a pendulum, Robert," she explained. "If you stop it from swinging in one direction, it can't have the momentum to swing in the other. Your blocking and avoiding the difficult feelings prevented you from experiencing the positive ones. If you aren't willing to feel the depths, you can never extend yourself to the heights of human experience."

Robert's heart pumped within his chest. He could feel the longing of intimacy striving to breach the barriers of pain and insecurity. "How do I let go?"

"Open up your heart to the pain," Helen said. "Feel the depth of it. Recognize it for what it is. Only then can you fully let go of it and open your heart to experiencing the love that is already there."

A strong arm wrapped itself around Robert's shoulders. "I'm here for you," his father's voice sounded in his ear. This was what he had needed all those years ago. Strength when he felt weak. Support when he was knocked down. He let down the walls and felt the flood of emotions wash over him.

Chapter 43

The Accident

June 1997

S andra drove home from the grocery store. It was a big step for her. It had been months since she had driven herself anywhere. Too many memories flashing through her mind. It was hard enough to get back in a car, let alone drive one. However, necessity outweighed comfort today. Tom was at work and wedding preparations couldn't wait.

She drove slowly. Every intersection felt like Russian roulette. Cars flashed in her peripheral only to vanish when she turned her head. Her knuckles gleamed white as she gripped the steering wheel. *You can do this,* she kept telling herself. She breathed a sigh of relief when she finally turned onto her street. No accident. She was safe.

At least I can *drive,* she thought. *Robert will never be able to drive again. Stuck in darkness and dependence.* The mental barrage of negativity returned. It was a common visitor. Any thought of Robert would bring it up instantly. The self-inflicted punishment wasn't helpful. She never felt any better and the guilt didn't subside, but she felt like she deserved it; so it continued.

As she put the groceries away, she thought about Robert sitting alone in his house. She imagined him eating one of the pre-prepared freezer meals she had purchased for him, food spilling onto the table as he brought each bite to his mouth.

A knock at the garage door startled her out of her thoughts. She turned to see Bobby's head poke through. "Hey, Mom!" His smile brightened the room. "You left the garage door open. Did you just get home?"

"I just picked up the stuff I needed for your reception on Saturday," Sandra said as she put the heavy whipping cream in the refrigerator. A broad, goofy smile spread across his face. Then he paused and his brow furrowed.

"Is Dad home?" Bobby asked.

"No," Sandra replied as she put the bag of confectioners sugar in the pantry.

"Then who drove you?"

"I drove myself," Sandra felt a surge of pride as she said it, but then felt immediately silly. She was a grown woman and had been driving for over thirty years. Of course she should be able to drive herself.

"Wow, Mom," Bobby said, eyebrows raised. "That's a big deal. How was it?"

"It was fine," she lied.

Bobby eyed her in disbelief. "Mom, you got nervous driving before the accident. And now you're trying to tell me that your first time driving yourself since then was fine?"

"Yes, Bobby," Sandra said without looking up from the groceries. "Your mom is a big girl, doing things all by herself."

"I didn't mean it like that, Mom," Bobby said. He picked up some cans of sweetened condensed milk and handed them to her. "I'm just impressed that you faced the trauma so quickly."

Sandra turned and looked at Bobby. "Well, you're important to me, so it was worth the risk. It wouldn't do to have a wedding reception without a cake."

Bobby grabbed his mother's hands and looked at them. He ran his thumbs over the scars that were finally starting to fade. "I'm just thankful you're alive to be at my wedding in the first place."

"Me too," Sandra said, pulling him into a hug. "Me too."

Sandra cringed internally. Those words played back in her head, only in Robert's voice. She felt his resentment weigh on her again. The picture of his face staring blankly back at her haunted her and threatened her happiness almost daily. As much as she tried to hide the sudden mood shift, when Bobby pulled away from the hug, she knew he noticed.

"What's the matter, Mom?" Bobby asked. He was such a perceptive boy.

"Nothing. I'm fine." She tried smiling one of her sunshine smiles, but it only came out partly cloudy.

"Mom, believe me, I can tell when you aren't fine, and this is one of those times. What happened?" He looked at her with a persistence she knew she wouldn't escape.

"Just had a little flashback." She knew she would need to give him just enough to sate his curiosity. She didn't need to tell him everything though. "I'll be fine, really. They just come randomly."

Bobby stared at her, holding her shoulders at arm's length. "You are a terrible liar, Mom. What's going on? This isn't about the accident, is it?"

She exhaled. What more could she give him without telling the whole story? "I'm just sad about Robert. He won't get to see your wedding."

"Ahh, Mom. This again? He's going to be at the wedding. He'll hear the whole thing. That's the most important part. You worry too much about him. It's not healthy."

She waited for more questioning, but Bobby seemed satisfied. No need to go into all the guilt and worry she felt every day. No reason to talk about how much she needed her brother to forgive her for the accident that had taken away his sight. Bobby didn't need to deal with that baggage. Not before his big day.

"I know," she went with it. "It's just hard sometimes."

Bobby pulled her back into a hug. "You are a good person, Mom."

"Thanks, Bobby." She said it, but she didn't feel it.

Sandra stared at the ceiling sleeplessly. Thoughts of Robert consumed her, taunting her sense of worth. Why did she struggle so much with her feelings of guilt? It was an accident—

and not even her fault for that matter. Yet the feeling of responsibility remained.

She rolled over, fitfully trying to find some comfortable position that would allow her mind to turn off long enough to fall asleep. Nothing worked. The dozens of times she tried every night for the past several weeks were evidence of that.

"Thinking about Robert again?" Tom whispered through the darkness.

"Yes," Sandra whispered back. "I feel trapped; held captive in some way. I keep trying to figure out the right thing to do or say that will make him forgive me."

Tom scooted closer to her and wrapped his arm around her waist. "If you thought about me every night as much as you think about him, our bed would be a much more exciting place. And you'd probably fall asleep faster too. You always do after we make—"

Sandra elbowed him in the gut. "Not funny, Tom." How he could come up with those stupid jokes in the middle of the night? Well, he was a man, so he was probably thinking about sex whenever the opportunity presented itself.

"Sorry, babe," she could feel him smiling at her. "It was just a suggestion."

"Not in the mood," she replied automatically. "I just don't know what to do anymore. It seems like nothing I do is ever enough."

"Sandra, what if he never forgives you?" Tom's tone was serious now. "Are you going to live the rest of your life this way? Sleepless nights and days filled with guilt and worry?"

"But he's my brother," Sandra protested. "He's the only family I have left."

"I'm not saying you need to abandon him. Just let go of the grip his personality has over you," Tom said, squeezing her.

"What do you mean?"

"Sandra," Tom said, "Robert is a bitter person. He is bound and determined to be miserable and to see all the negative things in his life. That's just him. He's been doing that as long as I've known him. You aren't going to change that. This isn't a new feature that developed when he went blind."

Sandra knew it was true. She couldn't remember a time that Robert didn't find a way to focus on the negative either. That didn't take away from his occasional thoughtfulness and humor, but he never could seem to notice all the good in his life.

"So, what do you think will change if he tells you he forgives you?" Tom asked.

"Well," Sandra thought for a moment. "I'd know that he's OK, and that *we're* OK. I'd know that he still cares about me and isn't holding some grudge against me."

"Do you think he doesn't care about you?"

"Well, no. I know he cares about me," Sandra realized.

"Can I tell you something straight?"

"Sure."

"You seem like you've placed yourself in some sort of mental prison and the only way out is for Robert to say he forgives you. But the reality is, you're the one holding yourself in that prison. You didn't do anything wrong. You were in an accident. It wasn't your fault. And you're probably the kindest, most thoughtful sibling I've ever known. You were that way before the accident, and you've been more so since. I think you need to forgive yourself more than anything else."

Again, he was right. She was beating herself up over everything that had happened. It was just hard having things out of her control. No matter how hard she tried, she couldn't change that. And now, her husband was suggesting something that was in her control, and she backed away from it like a poisonous serpent.

"And how do I do that?" Sandra turned and faced Tom.

"For starters, stop taking responsibility for things that aren't your responsibility. Robert forgiving you is his responsibility. You've already fulfilled your responsibility tenfold," Tom leaned in and kissed her.

"But I can't stop helping him out," Sandra retorted. "He needs me."

"I didn't say anything about stopping," Tom said slowly. "I was talking about why you're serving him. You can't be doing this so he'll forgive you. You'll just become resentful like him."

Something clicked in Sandra's mind. "You are a brilliant man, Thomas Newsom."

"Yes, that's true. I'm full of great ideas," Tom smiled and kissed Sandra again. "Which one are you referring to this time?"

"I can't make him forgive me, but that doesn't mean I should stop serving him. I serve him because I love him as my brother and for no other reason. I don't need to wear myself out finding the perfect act of service so he can say the words that for some reason I thought would make everything better. Even if he forgives me, he'll still be blind. I can't change that. But I will love and serve him."

Tom kissed Sandra and rolled her onto her back. "That's my girl! You're an amazing person. If Robert can't see that, well, then he is blind in more ways than one."

"I can't believe I didn't see this before," Sandra said, enjoying the pressure of Tom holding her tightly. "I feel liberated. Like I have a direction again. I can let him be him and just serve him anyways."

"I'm glad you can see it now. I was starting to get worried," Tom said. "Do you need some help falling asleep? I have another one of those brilliant ideas you were talking about."

"Hmm, tempting," Sandra said, flirtation heavy in her voice. "What did you have in mind?"

"Let me show you," Tom returned, kissing her lips with a softness that she couldn't resist.

Chapter 44

The Artwork

May 1984

The paint was finally dry. Robert worried that it was taking so long as the clock ticked towards the private showing. He wasn't used to how long the thicker brush strokes took to dry. Now, just in time, he could apply the varnish and let that dry before next week's event.

Robert pulled out the restoration-grade synthetic varnish and prepared the spray gun. He reflected on how much technology had changed this process since Adenet Dupuis had originally varnished this painting years ago. While a good varnish brings out the richness of all the colors, old varnishes yellowed with time, fading the original beauty. Now, these synthetic varnishes could last for at least one hundred years without yellowing at all. Robert loved that enduring quality to the preservation of each artwork he completed. It gave a sense of permanence to a tangible piece of history.

With the spray gun loaded, Robert carefully applied an even coat, spraying in vertical lines, up and down from left to right. Robert hated cutting a project so close to the line. To distract himself from the nagging sense of urgency, Robert absorbed himself in the newfound richness of color. He soaked himself in the complementary strokes of greens, blues, and purples with the ranges of hue and shade. He allowed himself to go into a deep, meditative state, placing his full attention into the nuance of each. The composition flowed through the cycle of light and shadow, drawing his attention through an unending loop. His breath synced with the rhythm of it all.

It was a masterpiece. He would miss the regular interaction and struggle he had with it. Now he hoped that others would be able to see the beauty as he did. Yet he knew they never could. So much of the joy was in the struggle. The wrestle of restoration. The return of what was lost.

Robert smiled. And waited.

Chapter 45

The Afterlife

Heaven had been majestic before, but as Robert wiped the tears from his cheeks, he was amazed by the sheer brilliance of it. Never before had he seen such luminance and richness. He was overwhelmed as his other senses tried to absorb what his eyes could not completely take in. There was such clarity in everything. He could see the finest details and comprehend it all without losing sight of the grander picture.

Love and joy emanated from everything. It was like he could see beyond the tangible form and into the spirit and soul of it. Everything was alive in its own way, serving a purpose and doing so in perfect harmony with everything around it.

"Thank you," Robert said as he tried to take it all in. "Thank you for loving me and helping me." He looked directly at both of his parents and could see and feel the depth of love that each of them had for him. Tears welled up in his eyes again. Despite the tears obscuring his vision, Robert recognized that he was seeing more clearly now than ever before.

"I should be the one to thank *you*," his father said, tears running down his cheeks as well. "You've given me something of immeasurable worth. Thank you for your forgiveness."

Father and son embraced, unbound from wounds, regrets, and resentments.

Helen stood in awe of this interaction between these two broken men. She gloried in the healing she was witnessing and recognized that the exchange had healed something in her heart as well. To see her husband and son loving and talking to each other filled a hole that had been there so long she had grown accustomed to it. With it filled, she recognized a similar hole for the same interchange between John and Sandra.

Helen smiled with anticipation. Her family would be whole again. What greater joy could be found than that?

Chapter 46

The Artwork

June 1984

He was nervous. Robert tried to tell himself this wasn't a date, but no amount of self-deception could alter the facts. He was dressed in a black suit and tie waiting at the doorstep of a woman to take her to an event for the first time in more years than he could remember.

He knocked again, worried that she may not have heard the first one. The door opened to reveal a woman that Robert almost didn't recognize. Her dress was vibrant sapphire blue and highlighted an attractive form he hadn't noticed before.

"Wow," Robert said. "You look great!"

Heather blushed. "Thank you. I hope it isn't too much."

"Well, people might think you're one of the artworks on display," Robert said. He felt uncomfortable with the emotions her surprising beauty was having on him. The last time he had allowed himself to feel this way didn't turn out well.

"Oh, stop," Heather shied away from the praise. "Should we go? We don't want to be late."

"Of course," Robert answered, extending his arm out for her. As they walked to the car, Robert's heart beat harder than he could imagine. He was prepared for the nervousness of the gallery and his restoration on display. He wasn't prepared for the feelings that Heather had stirred up in him. It felt dangerous.

The museum was buzzing with activity. It wasn't quite a red-carpet event, but there was a line of museum staff present to greet each attendee. Robert felt a bit out of place amid all the attention, but Heather seemed to be rolling with it.

Inside the museum, just outside the exhibit, a table was arrayed with catered hors d'oeuvres. People mingled, casually discussing individual artworks, pointing, and tipping their heads slightly as they did so. Robert and Heather filled a small plate with some food before joining the throng.

"Let me show you where they placed *The Garden Path*," Heather said, brightly smiling at Robert. "You're going to be thrilled."

Robert smiled back and followed her as she walked into the main exhibit. Beautiful paintings adorned the walls and Robert found himself slowing his pace, wanting to look more closely at each of them. Heather grabbed his hand and pulled him along into another room. There, centered on one of the walls, was the painting he had invested himself in for the past couple of months. It looked amazing and was lit perfectly.

"What do you think?" Heather asked.

"It's perfect," Robert answered.

"I thought so too," Heather said as she placed a small stuffed cracker in her mouth.

"Why such prominence?" Robert asked. "It isn't a famous painting by any means."

"The curator thought it was an excellent example of the French Impressionism of the period," she explained. "I think he also loved the story of it being found and restored. He thought it added to the romanticism of the piece. I agree with him. You've done a remarkable job with this one, Robert."

"Thank you," Robert whispered.

As they stood there, a group approached the painting. Robert listened in on their conversation, curious if any would notice the intensive restorative work. He hoped they wouldn't. His job was to make sure his work was not noticed.

"I love this one," a woman said to the man at her side. "The light and shadow bring out such wonderful color patterns."

The man nodded. "The sunbeam shining down through the trees is almost intoxicating," he replied. "The way it highlights the couple walking is masterful."

"I think that's the meaning of the painting," the woman commented.

"What do you mean?"

"The obvious focus is on the couple, or the relationship between them. They're walking along a path that is mostly in darkness and the main source of light in the whole painting is shining directly on them," the woman mused. "I think it shows the light and joy and importance of an intimate relationship."

The man nodded in agreement.

"I agree with them," Heather whispered to Robert.

Robert contemplated the assessment. He couldn't say that those thoughts hadn't come to his mind several times as he worked on it, but he chose instead to focus on the technical aspects of the restoration. But they were right. All elements of the painting drew attention to this one point. All else was in shadow. The light of life was found and illuminated in relationships.

Robert had shied away from the pain he felt in that light, only to find himself in darkness.

Chapter 47

The Afterlife

Robert walked with his father along the paths of perfectly manicured gardens. He saw others walking, conversing, and embracing. Some were still in the process of their own restoration, while those near them supported and guided them along. Robert allowed the love of those interactions to permeate his heart and elevate his love.

"Dad," Robert spoke to his father, "what was it like for you to wait for me to get here?"

John looked at his son with deep contemplation. "I had a lot of my own work to do before I was ready to meet you. A lot of healing and a lot of forgiving. But this was worth every minute of it. I can't explain the joy I feel with you now."

"I feel that too," Robert said. "I had the realization that I am thankful my sight wasn't immediately restored when I got here. The process gives it so much more value and meaning. I don't think it is possible to feel a fullness of joy any other way."

John nodded. "That's very true. I was nervous to see you because of the pain I knew I'd caused you. Facing the pain, as hard as it was, deepened my understanding of love. There's no place for fear in love. Only courage, humility and selflessness."

They stopped and sat in the shade of a weeping willow that formed a private alcove. Robert watched the thin, hanging branches sway in gentle unison as they tickled the tips of the lush green grass blades beneath.

"Mary isn't here yet," Robert commented.

"Are you ready to forgive her?" John asked.

"I think so," Robert answered. "I can differentiate between my own choices and hers now. I can see her as an individual, not just someone acting upon me. She'll have her own process, and I truly hope that goes well for her. Everyone deserves the healing that comes through forgiveness. I'm ready to give that to her."

John nodded thoughtfully. "I'm proud of you, son. I don't think I said that enough when you were young, but I want you to know it now."

"Thanks Dad, that means a lot."

They sat there in a peaceful silence, enjoying one another's company and presence. Father and son, relationship restored and enhanced.

"How long do you think Mom will take with Sandra?" Robert asked.

"As long as she needs," John answered. "Your mother's very intuitive. She'll let us know when Sandra's ready for us."

"I'm sure it'll be faster than I took," Robert predicted. "She was already filled with love and forgiveness. I'm just eager to tell her I'm sorry and that my blindness wasn't her fault. I should have done that years ago."

"You'll get the chance," John said. "And it'll be wonderful for both of you."

Robert looked in his father's face and could sense the pain of his anticipation. "She'll forgive you, Dad."

"I know, Robert. But that doesn't make the process easier. I still feel sadness at the pain I caused the two of you."

"I can understand that. I feel the same way about how I treated Sandra, especially because she was only ever good to me."

"We'll make it right together then," John said confidently.

The branches of the willow parted and bright light shined in on them. Helen's face peered in a moment later with a big smile across her face.

"She's ready now."

ABOUT THE AUTHOR

Nathan Sellers is a Licensed Clinical Social Worker working with youth and families to assist them in their therapeutic journey. He combines his passion of art, creativity, and therapy to write stories that inspire the reader toward self-discovery, healing, and growth. His blog, writingonpurpose.org, explores topics of trauma, relationships, communication, and finding meaning and purpose in one's life.

Made in the USA
Las Vegas, NV
09 December 2021